JUSTICE

AN OLIVIA MILLER MYSTERY BOOK 4

J. A. WHITING

To hear about new books and book sales, please sign up for my mailing list at:

www.jawhitingbooks.com

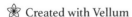 Created with Vellum

For my family, with love

1

Olivia and Brad left their seats in Section 24 of Boston's Fenway Park and followed the people streaming out of the stands to exit the ballpark. The Prudential building rose up in the distance against the dark night sky and music blared from the speakers to celebrate the team's win.

Olivia held her boyfriend's hand and a wide grin spread over her face. "That was awesome."

"Best thing I've been to in a long time," Brad agreed. "My ears are buzzing from all the cheering."

Olivia's blue eyes were bright. "I know. It was crazy." She leaned over and kissed Brad. "I'm happy," she told him, her eyes sparkling.

Brad touched the side of Olivia's face and

beamed at her. "We're really lucky that Ynes gave us those tickets."

Olivia had met Ynes Clinton at university and they'd become friends during their senior year of studies when a difficult incident welded a strong and special bond between them. Ynes, Olivia, and some others had discovered a gruesome murder scene at an off-campus apartment during the fall of their last year of college and the group of friends worked together to help discover the killer.

Ynes, close in age to Olivia, was bright, funny, and athletic. Her long, straight, ebony hair complemented her light olive skin and dark brown eyes. Ynes spent the first five years of her life in the Boston area before moving to London with her stepfather and stepbrother. She recently had been studying for her master's degree at Oxford University, and from June through September, had worked in Washington, D.C. doing research. Visiting Massachusetts for two weeks, she planned to stay with a friend on Cape Cod for two days before going to Boston to see her aunt and then meeting up with Olivia.

Ynes's aunt had won two tickets to the Red Sox game along with five nights accommodation at a Boston hotel. The aunt offered the tickets to Ynes explaining that she would rather die than attend a loud, boring Boston sporting event. Ynes had no interest in baseball and offered the tickets and hotel to Olivia who gladly accepted.

"How about a drink at the Cask and Flagon?" Brad asked.

Olivia smiled, but shook her head. "We'll never get in, too crowded."

"You're probably right," he said, "but, let's go see anyway. If we can't get in, we'll go someplace else." As they joined the throng of people heading out to the street, a text came in to Olivia's phone, but she didn't hear it over the noise in the stadium.

Brad and Olivia strolled hand in hand, weaving and dodging around the mass of fans and then turned right onto Brookline Avenue.

"Oh, no," Brad said when he saw the line of patrons waiting to get into the bar.

"Plan B?" Olivia asked. A light breeze ruffled her long, light brown hair.

"How about we walk up to Boylston Street? Maybe there will be less people up that way."

Olivia nodded. As they walked along Lansdowne, Olivia pulled out her phone to check her messages and she halted in her tracks, a flash of anxiety rushing through her body.

Brad turned to see why she'd stopped.

Olivia held up her phone's screen so Brad could read the text message.

I need your help I'll explain later

"It's from Ynes." Olivia's forehead pinched with worry. Her fingers flew over the phone's screen to reply to the message.

"What could be wrong?" Brad asked.

Olivia shrugged. "That's what I asked her."

"Maybe her train broke down," Brad said. Ynes was supposed to be on the train back to Boston from her visit to Cape Cod.

Brad had to return home to Ogunquit, Maine in the morning, but Olivia was staying in the city for two more days so that she and Ynes could spend time together, go to lunch, and tour some museums.

Olivia said, "I hope she's not stuck in a broken-down train somewhere." Crossing Massachusetts Ave, she and Brad continued up Boylston Street.

"Why doesn't she answer my text?" Olivia checked her phone for the third time.

"Maybe call her," Brad suggested.

Olivia pressed some buttons on the screen and held the phone to her ear. After several seconds, she raised her eyes to Brad and shook her head. "She isn't picking up."

"Maybe she was able to reach someone else and got the help she needed?" Brad said. "Or maybe the train is stuck some place that has no cell service."

"Maybe." Olivia's face was lined with concern.

"She must be okay, otherwise she'd try you again." Brad put his arm around Olivia's shoulders. "Our team just won a great game. We need to celebrate."

"You're right. Ynes must be fine or she'd text me again. Let's go." Olivia reached over and squeezed Brad's hand as they headed up the sidewalk, the lights of the city shimmering around them.

WHEN OLIVIA WOKE, she reached for her phone on the bedside table. There were still no messages from Ynes. Brad was curled up under the blanket, so Olivia decided to shower and let him sleep a bit longer.

When she stepped out of the bathroom and saw that her boyfriend was still snoozing, Olivia dressed quietly and left to go down to the restaurant for some breakfast to bring back up to their room.

Fifteen minutes later she opened their hotel room door carrying the take-out containers.

Brad stirred in the bed. "What's this?" He yawned and stretched. "Smells delicious. You're up early."

Olivia placed the bag of food on the round table next to the windows and sat down next to Brad on the bed to kiss him.

"I woke up early. I thought I'd grab some breakfast for us so we could eat here. I hope you're hungry because I bought a lot." She smiled as she ran her fingers through his mussed hair.

Brad grabbed her hand and kissed each one of her fingers. "I'm starving."

"Come on then." Olivia went to the table and removed the boxes of food from the bag. "There are eggs and bacon. Pancakes and berries. I got two blueberry scones with butter and coffee and tea." She looked over at Brad with an impish grin. "That should be enough for me. What are you going to eat?"

"Very funny." Brad pulled on his sweatpants and sat down in one of the plush chairs next to the table laden with the breakfast items. "Looks like a beautiful day," he said looking out the window which provided a lovely view of the Boston skyline. "I wish

I could stay, but it's probably for the best that I need to head home. You haven't seen Ynes for a year. You've got some catching up to do."

"I really can't wait to see her." Olivia placed eggs and bacon in front of Brad. She lifted one of the pancakes and some of the berries onto his plate along with a scone, and then put his coffee and some creamers next to his plate. "That ought to hold you for a while." With a smile, she sat down in the matching chair to dig into the pancakes with berries and a cup of tea.

"There still isn't a text from Ynes." Olivia lifted her tea cup to her lips.

Brad looked up from his breakfast. "She must be at her aunt's house."

"I don't know." Worry lines creased Olivia's forehead. "She was supposed to text me this morning about where to meet her for lunch."

"It's early. There's still time to hear from her. Did you text her when you got up?"

"I will right now." Olivia lifted her phone and sent off a short message.

When Brad finished eating, he took a shower while Olivia read the news on his laptop. Brad stepped from the bathroom toweling his hair.

"There's still no reply from Ynes." Olivia's eyes were on the laptop screen.

"Do you know her aunt's address?" Brad dressed and combed his hair.

"I know her name. Ynes said she lived on Beacon Hill."

"Do a search on the aunt's name. See if an address comes up," Brad said.

"What are you thinking?" Olivia asked. "You think I should go to the house if I don't hear from her?" She tapped the laptop keys to search Ynes's aunt's name.

"I doubt the aunt would mind if you showed up on her doorstep."

"Here it is," Olivia said. "A phone number, too. I'll call." She punched the number into her phone and while she listened to it ring, she wrote the woman's address on a small pad of paper that was on the desk.

Olivia raised her eyes to Brad. "It's gone to voicemail. What should I do?"

Brad buttoned up his shirt and pulled a sweater over his head. "They could have gone out shopping or for breakfast. You wanted to take a walk anyway. Why don't we head over to Beacon Hill before I have to leave and stop by the house? See if they've come back."

With anxiety pricking at her, Olivia agreed. They gathered up their jackets and headed to the elevator.

Stepping outside into the bright October sunshine, Olivia and Brad strolled up Newbury Street, stopped to browse in a few stores, and then entered the Public Garden. Following the paths that wound around the pond, the two walked past Weeping Willow trees and garden plots full of colorful chrysanthemums.

People pushed baby strollers, walked dogs, and jogged through the park. Olivia and Brad held hands as they passed the bronze *Make Way for Ducklings* statues. They waited on the corner, crossed Beacon Street, headed down Chestnut, and into the Beacon Hill area of Boston.

Olivia used a map on her phone to find where Ynes's aunt's street was located. "We should turn right up ahead, follow that street to the top, then turn left. The building should be right there," she said.

Climbing the hill, they found Ynes's aunt's brownstone. Flower boxes sat at the base of each of the windows filled with tiny pumpkins, mums, and greens. Two bronze planters spilling over with greens and flowers stood at each side of the front landing at the top of the granite steps.

"This is it," Brad said. "It's a beautiful building."

They walked up the steps to the glossy, black, front door with a brass knocker set in the middle. Olivia pressed the doorbell to the left of the entrance.

"Brad, look. The door isn't shut all the way." Olivia's voice began to tremble. The massive door was open a crack.

Brad glanced down and grabbed Olivia's elbow. "What's that?"

Olivia followed his gaze to the door's threshold and her heart jumped into her throat. "Blood?" she gasped.

Olivia put her hand against the door and pushed it open. Bloody footprints smeared the foyer's white marble floor.

"Look at the floor." Olivia lifted her foot to enter the home. "Ynes?"

"Liv, no." Brad pulled her back. "Don't go inside."

Olivia leaned forward from the front landing, her eyes flashing about the foyer. A dark wooden staircase stood to the right and a fully lit cut-glass chandelier hung from the ceiling. An ornately carved wooden side table was placed on the left wall of the foyer with a mirror on the wall above it. A glass vase was set on the middle of the table filled with an array of large stem, dark-orange gladiolus.

A white box wrapped with a red ribbon lay on the floor just inside the entrance as if someone had dropped it or threw it there. Gold letters were embossed in the upper left corner of the box with a return address: Linden Leather Goods, Boston, MA. In the center of the box was a label printed with the name: *Abigail Millett* and the address of the brownstone.

"Brad, what's happened?" Olivia croaked. "Ynes!"

Brad pulled his phone from his jacket pocket and punched in "911."

After standing together on the front landing for five minutes, they heard a car's engine and turned to see a Boston Police car pulling up to the curb.

"There's blood in the foyer!" Olivia shouted to them. "Hurry!"

Two officers emerged from their vehicle, their hands on their weapons. "Step away from the door," one officer ordered. "Keep your hands where we can see them."

"There's blood inside the front entry," Olivia told them again.

She and Brad raised their hands and moved down the steps to the sidewalk.

"We just got here," Brad said. "We rang the bell. The door was ajar. We could see the blood on the threshold and on the foyer floor."

Olivia clutched Brad's arm. Her heart pounded and her vision twinkled. "I need to sit down," she whispered and slid to the brick sidewalk onto her butt.

She rested her head against her knees as Brad knelt down beside her and took her hand.

2

B rad and Olivia reported to the officer why they were standing at the front door of the Beacon Hill brownstone. More police arrived to the scene. The coroner's car pulled up along with detectives and a crime scene unit.

Inside the brownstone, the body of a middle-aged woman had been found on her back on the floor of the living room. She had been stabbed multiple times.

Ynes was not in the house.

"My friend was planning to stay with her aunt for the rest of the week," Olivia told the detective. "She was supposed to arrive last night." Olivia showed the officer the text that she had received from Ynes indicating that she needed help. "I had plans to meet her for lunch today."

"We were concerned," Brad said. "So we walked over to see if Ynes was here."

A detective asked more questions, took Olivia and Brad's contact information, and told them he would be in touch. They were free to go.

"He wasn't very forthcoming with any information," Brad said as they walked along the brick sidewalk.

"I guess he isn't allowed to share anything," Olivia said. "They mustn't know much yet."

"I'm sure we'll be hearing from them. I don't think they're done with us," Brad said.

"I'm pretty shook up." Olivia rubbed her temples with shaking fingers. "Can we go back to the hotel?" Over the past year and a half, Olivia had been involved with two crimes; one recent, regarding the death of her aunt, and the other, a forty-year-old cold case investigation into the homicide of her two cousins ... and she'd hoped never to have anything to do with murder ever again.

When they arrived at the hotel and took the elevator to their room, Olivia plopped down on the bed and rested back against the pillow.

Brad took a bottle of water from the mini bar and poured some into a glass for her. "Need anything, Liv?" He sat next to her and rubbed her arm.

Olivia sipped the water and shook her head. "I just want to talk. What do you think is going on? Where is Ynes?"

The room phone rang and Olivia jumped. "Maybe this is her now."

Brad leaned to the bedside table and lifted the phone's receiver, listened, and then looked at Olivia. "Yes?" He paused, still holding the phone to his ear. "Yes. Okay. We'll come down to the lobby in few minutes."

Olivia sat up and watched him with a quizzical look.

Brad replaced the receiver. "It was the front desk. They said that someone was asking for us and they put him on the line. The man said his name was Michael White and he was Ynes Clinton's friend and that she sent him over to the hotel to get in touch with us. I told him we would come down to the lobby."

Olivia looked at Brad with a blank expression. "Ynes never mentioned anyone named Michael White to me."

"Maybe it just never came up."

"I don't know," Olivia said skeptically.

"Well, he knew our names and that we were staying here as guests of Ynes. Who else would have told him?" Brad asked.

Olivia got up from the bed. "Let's go see what he has to say. But let's not give him any information."

The elevator doors opened to reveal the busy hotel lobby. Olivia and Brad exited the elevator and scanned the people for the man who claimed to be Ynes's friend.

Olivia spotted a dark-haired man rise from one of the leather sofas which were arranged in clusters around the room.

The man, who looked to be in his late thirties or early forties, was tall and olive skinned. His shirt and slacks were well-fitted in a European cut. He made eye contact with Brad and Olivia as they walked towards him.

"Olivia? Brad?" the man asked.

"Yes." Olivia nodded.

They shook hands.

"Michael White." When he introduced himself, the man spoke with a slight English accent. "Can you sit for a minute?" He indicated the sofa.

Olivia and Brad sat side by side on the brown leather couch and White took a seat in a club chair across from them. "Ynes asked me to pick up the suitcase she left with you."

Olivia sat straighter, leveling a suspicious gaze at

the man across from her. Ynes had checked into the hotel room before Olivia and Brad arrived in order to leave her large suitcase there so she wouldn't have to drag it to Cape Cod with her. *Ynes never mentioned this man to me. Why would she send someone to pick up her suitcase without informing me?* "But we don't have her suitcase," Olivia lied. "Ynes changed her mind. She decided to take her bags with her."

"Did she? She didn't tell me," White said. He looked puzzled. "Why did she change her mind?"

"I don't know." Olivia looked pointedly at White. "Ynes didn't tell me you were coming by to get her bag."

"She didn't mention me?"

Olivia shook her head. "When did you last hear from her?"

"Last evening," White said.

"I've been trying to reach her," Olivia said. "We had plans to meet for lunch today."

White said, "I didn't know that. I was supposed to pick her up at the rail station today, but she hasn't texted me. She said she would let me know if the train was on time or not."

"Ynes told me she was coming into Boston *last* night," Olivia said.

"Last night?" White's eyebrows knitted together.

"Was she planning to stay here with you?"

"No. She was going to her aunt's house," Olivia said.

White's face took on a confused expression. "Ynes doesn't have an aunt in Boston."

Brad and Olivia exchanged a quick glance.

"Are we talking about the same person?" Olivia asked.

A smile flashed over White's face for a second before realizing that Olivia wasn't joking. "Ynes Clinton. Tall ... long black hair. Attractive."

"Ynes told me she would be staying at her aunt's home on Beacon Hill for two weeks," Olivia said. "She was supposed to arrive last night."

"Two weeks?" White said. "I'm supposed to be flying out tomorrow."

Brad looked at Olivia then turned back to White and said, "Something happened at her aunt's house."

White's brows furrowed and he shook his head. "There is no aunt. Ynes doesn't have an aunt in Boston."

Olivia's eyes scanned White's face trying to gauge his sincerity. He seemed honest in what he was saying, but Olivia had felt pricks of distrust throughout the conversation.

"Where are you from?" she asked.

"England. Oxford. I'm a doctoral student at the university."

"When did you arrive in the States?"

"A week ago. I flew into Washington, D.C."

"Why are you visiting the States?" Olivia asked.

White stiffened and when he answered his voice had an edge to it. "I had some business in Washington. I visited with Ynes, then she came up here. She had someone she wanted to see on Cape Cod. She's meeting me so I can spend the day with her and do some shopping before I fly home." He looked from Brad to Olivia. "I'm supposed to pick up her bag," he said firmly.

"We don't have it." Olivia kept her face blank even though she bristled with tension. "Is Ynes planning to meet me?"

"I don't know. Our communication has been short. She asked me to get her bag from you and she said she'd call me later."

"You might want to go to the Boston Police department," Brad said.

A red flush tinged White's neck and creeped up to his cheeks. "Perhaps that's the best idea. In order to recover Ynes's property."

"I meant because of her aunt," Brad said. "There was a problem at the house."

"There is no aunt." White spoke with a loud voice and some of the hotel patrons turned to look in their direction.

"It's serious," Brad said, his voice low. "What happened at the house. You should go talk to the police."

Olivia pulled out her phone. She wasn't going to tell White about Ynes's text from last night reporting that she needed help. "What number do you have for Ynes? Maybe I punched in her number incorrectly. One of us should call her and have her straighten this out."

White stood. "I don't know what's going here. I don't know you. I'm certainly not going to give you Ynes's number. I'll speak with her and she can clear this up. I'm sorry to have taken your time." He wheeled and stormed out of the lobby.

The doorman opened the large glass door and White hurried through.

Brad turned to Olivia. "What the heck was that about?"

"I don't know." Olivia looked through the huge windows of the lobby to the bustling streets of Boston. "But, I don't like it."

Justice

3

Olivia had put Ynes's large suitcase into Brad's trunk so they could drive it over to the aunt's house once her friend arrived. "We need to get Ynes's bag from the trunk of the car. I don't want to leave it in there," Olivia said. "But, we don't want anyone to see us with it."

Brad was sitting on the bed of their hotel room hunched over his laptop. "Liv, are you being dramatic?"

"Am I?" Olivia rustled through her purse. "Was I being dramatic when I knew Aggie didn't die from a heart attack?" she asked softly. Two summers ago, the authorities in Ogunquit had labeled Olivia's aunt's death a cardiac arrest, but Olivia was full of suspicions about what really had happened and did not rest until she discovered the truth.

Brad lifted his eyes to Olivia. "So what are you thinking about what's going on here?"

"I have no idea, but my intuition tells me not to trust that White guy. And where is Ynes? Her aunt has been murdered." Olivia carried her purse to the bed and sat next to Brad. She dumped the contents onto the blanket. "I can't find the valet ticket."

Brad lifted his wallet out of his back pocket and pulled the valet ticket from the billfold.

"Oh," Olivia said. "You have it."

"I'm not discounting your intuition," Brad said. "You've been right lots of times before. And there's plenty of reason for suspicion ... Ynes's aunt is dead, this guy trying to pick up Ynes's bag, Ynes being out of contact." Brad reached for Olivia's hand. "Let's talk it out. Let's not allow the strange experiences we've had in the past color what's going on now. Let's think things through logically."

When a sudden thought popped into Olivia's mind, her eyes widened and her voice shook. "Could Ynes have been kidnapped? What if she was at the aunt's house when someone broke in? They could have killed the aunt and taken Ynes." Olivia jumped up. "We shouldn't have put her suitcase in the trunk of the car. Someone might try to break into it. Someone might have broken in already." She hurried across the room and grabbed the keys from the desk. "Come on. We need to hurry."

"We shouldn't panic."

"I'm not panicking. I'm being cautious. Did you find anything unusual on the internet about Ynes?"

"Not yet." Brad shook his head.

Olivia's eyes narrowed. "Does she go to Oxford like she claims to? Did she actually work in D.C these past months?"

"I didn't get that far."

"What's going on?" Olivia muttered as she turned and yanked the door of the hotel room open. "Come on."

Brad followed her into the hallway. Olivia passed the elevator and made for the entrance to the stairwell.

"Why the stairs? The valet is at the front door," Brad asked.

"I changed my mind. I don't want the valet. I don't want the valet to see us take the bag out of the car ... if the bag is still in the car. We need to go straight down to the garage." Olivia jogged down the stairs with Brad trotting behind, rushing down the steps, flight after flight.

"The elevator would have been faster," Brad said between breaths.

When they reached the entrance door to the parking garage, Olivia stopped.

"What is it?" Brad asked.

"There's a fire alarm." She pointed to the wall. "I think I should go to the car alone. I'm smaller than you. I can move between the cars with less chance of detection. If I scream, then set off the fire alarm."

"No. For Pete's sake. I'm not going to stand here while you go to the car alone." Brad ran his hand through his hair. "What am I saying? No one is after us. No one is looking for us."

Olivia's eyes bored into Brad's. "How does that guy claiming to be Ynes's friend know we're supposed to have her bag? Someone might be after Ynes's belongings. Where is she? If she's okay, why doesn't she contact me? Who is that Michael White guy? Why did someone kill her aunt?"

Brad blew out a long breath and raised one eyebrow. "Ynes doesn't have an aunt, remember? According to her friend."

"If she doesn't have an aunt then who was that dead woman on Beacon Hill? Ynes gave me that woman's name and address. Aunt or no aunt, Ynes knows her. Well, she knew her."

"It wouldn't hurt for us to be careful, I guess." Brad gave in to Olivia's evidence.

"Exactly." Olivia put her hand on the door handle. "If I scream…"

"No way." Brad nudged Olivia aside. "If *I* scream, *you* pull the fire alarm."

"Okay." Olivia smiled and tried to lighten the mood by teasing Brad. "You're too tall. Hunch down, but don't be obvious that you're trying to be inconspicuous."

"Yeah, hunching down won't call any attention to me," Brad deadpanned.

"Go." Olivia nodded.

Brad opened the door and entered the garage. The place was empty.

Olivia held the door to the garage open a crack so she could watch him.

After walking the length of a line of parked vehicles, Brad darted to his car positioned against the far wall. He opened the trunk and pulled out a large black suitcase. Olivia sighed with relief when she saw him moving towards her across the garage lot with the case. She pulled the door open for him.

"Thank heavens," she said and turned for the stairs.

"The elevator's this way." Brad pointed.

Olivia shook her head. "We don't want anyone to see us."

"I'm not carrying this thing up all those flights of stairs. It weighs a ton."

Olivia stared at him. "I'll take it."

"Ugh," Brad groaned as he held on to the suitcase and followed Olivia up the first flight.

THEY MADE it back to their hotel room undetected. Brad puffed from carrying the heavy bag up so many flights of stairs. Olivia passed the key card over the security device above the handle of their room. The little light turned green and she opened the door.

Olivia stopped in her tracks. "Brad." Her voice was tight.

Brad looked over Olivia's shoulder into the room. Everything had been overturned and items were strewn all over the carpet. The mattress was askew, hanging partly off its platform. The contents of their two small suitcases had been emptied onto the floor.

"Oh, hell," Brad moaned.

Olivia took Brad's arm to keep him from going into the room and quickly shut the door. "Someone could be hiding in there," she said in a hushed tone. She pointed down the hall and whispered. "Back to the stairs."

They hustled down the corridor and entered the stairwell.

"We need to tell the front desk what happened," Brad said.

"We will. Just, not now." Olivia took out her phone.

"What are you doing?"

"We need to check into a different hotel. We shouldn't stay here. And we can't use our credit cards in case someone is monitoring us."

"We aren't secret agents, you know," Brad said. "No one cares about us."

"We weren't gone from the room very long. Somebody must be watching us."

"It could be a coincidence." Brad leaned against the wall and thought out loud. "Someone broke into our room right after we left to go down to the garage. Maybe someone *is* looking for Ynes's luggage."

Olivia nodded and pressed on her phone to place the call. "Joe." For more than twenty years, Joe Hanson had lived next door to Olivia and Aggie's home in Ogunquit and he had been Aggie's long-time boyfriend. Joe had always been like a father to Olivia.

When Olivia spoke, her voice was low as she told Joe what had happened and what she needed. When she ended the call, she turned to Brad. "Joe is going to reserve a room for us at the Colonnade Hotel using his credit card. I'll call for a car and have it meet us in the alley in back. Olivia placed the call and the two of them walked to the alley behind the building.

WHEN THEY WERE FINALLY in the new hotel room, they collapsed into the two plush chairs.

"I'll call the hotel in a minute to report the break-in," Brad said as he leaned back in the chair. "I hope they didn't steal my laptop."

"Probably, not. I think they're only looking for Ynes's stuff," Olivia said. "Who knows why?"

Brad perked up. "Let's look."

"What?"

"Let's open her suitcase. See what's so important," Brad said.

"That would be snooping."

"Since she's missing in action, I think we have cause to search her bag. Anyway, she left it with us. We have a duty to protect it so we need to see what we're protecting."

"Why do we?" Olivia's head tilted in question.

"So we know how much effort is necessary to protect it."

"It seems wrong to go through her things," Olivia said.

"Desperate times," Brad said. "Is there a key?"

"No, it's a code. 5-7-4."

Brad put the large piece of luggage on the floor and turned the dials to match the code. He clicked the metal latch and flicked it up and then unzipped the suitcase and gently lifted the lid. "Clothes," Brad said.

Olivia knelt beside the bag. She gingerly removed a silk shirt and a black skirt. She rustled through the items feeling for anything unusual.

Brad scooped the clothes onto the floor with two handfuls.

"I could have done that," Olivia said. "I was trying to keep things in order so I could put it all back the way it was. I feel awful looking through her stuff."

There was a zippered compartment on the inside of the luggage. Brad tugged on the zipper and reached inside. He removed what looked like a makeup case and handed it to Olivia while he searched the other inside pockets.

Olivia unsnapped the case. "Brad." Her voice was soft.

Brad looked up.

Olivia tilted the case in her hands so that he could see.

"What the..." Brad said. He took the case and slipped the contents out onto the carpet between them.

There was a British passport with a picture of a blond Ynes and with a variation of her name printed on it, Y. Ella Cohen. There was a credit card for the different name. A leather wallet contained one hundred dollar bills. Lots of them. A small zippered bag held three computer USB flash drives. Two phones lay in the mix of stuff.

Brad and Olivia stared at each other.

"What does it mean?" Olivia asked. Her face was creased with worry.

"Well...she could be some sort of a government agent. Or, maybe ... a criminal." Brad brushed his hand over the things. "Maybe she's in a witness protection program?"

"Ugh." Olivia's shoulders slumped. "What's going on? I know Ynes has dual citizenship, but why is she using her middle name as her main name? And why is she blond?"

They stared at the items on the floor.

"Let's check the bottom of the bag," Olivia suggested.

"What are we going to find next?" Brad groaned.

They peered into the bag and found two pairs of shoes, two scarves, a makeup case containing only makeup, and a case with some costume jewelry inside. Olivia slid her hand around the bottom of the bag.

"There's something else." She removed a leather case and held it out to Brad. "Want to do the honors?"

Brad pulled the zipper and removed something from the case.

Olivia gasped.

Brad held a knife. A big one. He placed it on the floor pointing the tip away from them and they sat in silence for several minutes.

"What do we do with all this?" Brad asked.

"The passport with a different name," Olivia said. "The credit card and all that cash? A knife. Why does she have all of these things?"

"Should we bring it to the police?" Brad asked.

"I don't know," Olivia said. Her head was spinning. "Maybe we should just pack it all back like it was, lock it, and wait for Ynes to contact us."

Brad was quiet while he thought it over.

"What if she's in law enforcement?" Olivia asked. "She could be an FBI agent or in the CIA or Scotland Yard or something. We wouldn't want to blow her cover. I think we should wait a while longer before we go to the police."

"Why would she ask us to carry this stuff for her?" Brad asked.

Olivia shrugged and then made eye contact with her boyfriend. "What if she *wanted* us to find all of this? Why else would she give me the combination? Why would I ever need it? She must have wanted us to be able to get into the suitcase."

"Why would she want us to open the luggage? Why would she think we would ever open her suitcase?" Brad asked. "What circumstances would ever warrant us opening her bag?"

"The ones that just happened," Olivia said.

THEY WIPED the knife down with a cloth to remove their fingerprints from it and then packed all of the things back the way they'd found them and locked the piece of luggage.

"What should we do with it?" Olivia asked. "We can't risk keeping it in the car."

"We'll have to leave it here where we can keep an eye on it. Hopefully no one followed us."

"I guess that's our only option," Olivia said.

"Let's go back to the hotel and tell them about the break-in," Brad said. "Then why don't we both head home."

"I know you need to get back," Olivia said slowly, "but I think I'm going to stay here for a couple of days like I'd planned. I want to be here if Ynes calls and wants to see me."

"I don't think you should stay," Brad told her.

"Nobody cares about me. It's this bag someone is after."

Brad knew there was no talking Olivia out of an idea once it was in her head. "I'll take the suitcase back with me. I can keep it safe and you won't have it here in the room to put you in danger. When I leave, you should go out for a couple of hours in case someone knows where we are and breaks in to check for the bag. They'll see it isn't here and then they'll leave you alone."

Olivia smiled. "Good idea."

4

———————

Brad and Olivia entered the first hotel they'd stayed at and stopped at the front desk to report the break in to their room. Hotel security escorted them up to the room where they went through their things to determine if anything was missing. All of their belongings were in the room including Brad's laptop which had been tossed on the floor, but was still working. The police were called and they took Brad and Olivia's statements. The hotel management offered them an upgraded room, but they declined. They gathered their things and headed to the lobby to check out.

The desk clerk handed them the room receipt and an envelope with *Ms. Miller* typed on the front. "This was left for you."

Olivia took it. "For me? Who left it?"

"A delivery man brought it in not long ago."

Olivia turned the letter over in her hand. "But it isn't in a delivery envelope."

The hotel clerk stared at the letter.

"Was it removed from a UPS or FedEx package?" Olivia asked.

"No, we would never do that," the clerk said. "A courier delivered it."

Olivia and Brad walked to one of the lobby sofas next to the window.

"What's this about?" Brad asked.

Olivia opened the envelope. She pulled out a ticket and a paper receipt. Olivia's eyes narrowed. "Look at this." She held the ticket up for Brad to see. A first class airline ticket from Boston to Washington, D.C. in Olivia's name.

"What the...?" Brad said. "What's the paper say?"

"It's a hotel reservation. Fully paid for. In Alexandria." Olivia raised her eyes to Brad.

"Do you think it's a joke?" Brad asked. He took the ticket from Olivia. "The flight leaves tomorrow morning."

"It's a pretty expensive joke," Olivia said.

They sat in silence for a minute.

"Somebody wants me in D.C.," Olivia said.

Brad blew out a long breath.

Olivia said, "It's Ynes. Her text said she needed help."

"She must need a hell of a lot of help to pay for you to fly to D.C.," Brad said. "Are you going?"

"Should I?"

With a sigh, Brad said, "I guess you should go and see what this is about. If someone was going to hurt you, they would have done it here, now … no need to bring you all the way to D.C. It has to be Ynes who wants you there." He paused and sucked in a breath. "You trust her, Liv?"

Olivia nodded and said softly, "With my life."

RELUCTANTLY, Brad left the city to return to his bookstore in Maine.

In the quaint seaside town, Olivia ran an antique shop that had previously belonged to her aunt. After inheriting the cottage her Aunt Aggie owned, Olivia decided to rent it out and live in the small apartment over the shop. An older woman named Rose had been renting the house and Olivia hired her to work in the antique store. Rose said she'd be happy to run the place until the young woman returned.

Standing on the sidewalk watching Brad drive

away from her, Olivia's heart sank as a sensation of being adrift on a stormy sea washed over her making her feel tiny ... and alone in a dangerous world.

Olivia had called Joe to tell him what was happening and that she would be going to Washington, D.C. for a few days to hopefully see Ynes. Despite some misgivings, Joe agreed that it was important for Olivia to help her friend.

Before Brad left the city to head home, Olivia told him what she'd noticed in Ynes's aunt's foyer. "The box on the foyer floor at the brownstone was from a leather goods shop in the Fenway area. From the position of the box on the floor, it seemed to have been dropped or tossed there, not placed on the floor. I wonder if whoever delivered it saw something. I wonder if the box was delivered before the woman was killed ... or while the attack was in progress."

"How do you know where the box came from?" Brad asked.

"The business address was on it. It was right there in front of us on the floor. It was for Abigail Millett."

"If anybody from the leather shop saw anything, I doubt they'll tell you. I would think they'd be frightened by what they saw and they sure wouldn't talk to a stranger about it. They won't trust an unknown person off the street to confide in," Brad had said.

"I just want to see what they say," Olivia told him.

Olivia found the leather shop, opened the door, and stepped into a well-stocked front room with shelves and display tables of shoes, cowboy boots, handbags, briefcases, wallets, and backpacks. As she moved around the space, Olivia ran her hand admiringly over the soft leather of a gray purse just as an older woman emerged from the back workroom.

"May I help you?" The woman, in her sixties, was tall and thin with blond hair streaked with gray. She wore it up in a loose bun. Her brown eyes shone with intelligence. She smoothed the skirt of her navy blue dress. "I'm Paulina."

"I have a friend whose aunt purchased something from your shop. The woman's name is Abigail Millett. She lives in Beacon Hill. Do you know her?" Olivia watched the woman and noticed a flash of something pass over her face.

"Millett? We have a number of clients who live in Beacon Hill." Paulina moved a few steps closer, keeping her face neutral.

"I think Ms. Millett was supposed to get a delivery yesterday," Olivia said. "Do you use a delivery service to bring goods to your customers in the Boston area?"

"Why do you ask?" The older woman gave Olivia a pleasant smile. "Are you interested in shipping something you purchase?"

Olivia decided to be upfront. "My friend is concerned. Something happened at her aunt's brownstone yesterday, something serious. A box from your shop was on the foyer floor of the home. We wondered if whoever delivered the box might have seen or heard anything."

Several emotions seemed to fly over the woman's face in a matter of a second, but before Paulina could speak, Olivia noticed someone standing at the threshold of the workroom.

A man in his late thirties, tall, with a stocky build and dark brown hair stood quietly listening to the conversation. He wore a scuffed leather apron and held a leather-working tool in his hand.

The older woman followed Olivia's gaze and turned around. "Oh, Randy. It's okay. You can go back to work."

The man stood there staring at Olivia with curiosity.

When Olivia took a few steps forward, the man

seemed to shrink into himself so she stopped and introduced herself.

The man looked at her, but he didn't speak. His brown eyes resembled Paulina's in size, shape, and color.

Paulina said, "This is my son, Randy. He's nonverbal. He does most of the leather production. He's a very talented artist." She nodded at her son. "It's okay. You can go back to your table."

The man didn't move. He kept his eyes pinned on Olivia.

"He's slightly *off* today," the woman whispered. "He doesn't usually want to interact with customers."

"Did you make all of these?" Oliva asked softly and gestured to a display table of cowboy boots.

Randy shifted his head a little to take a quick look at the boots.

"They're beautiful." Olivia smiled.

"The boots are custom made by Randy," the woman said. "We sell a lot of boots to Boston sports stars and other local celebrities. Randy loves sports. It's a thrill for him when one of the players comes in to order a pair and get fitted."

"I can see why you're in demand," Olivia said to the man. "These are really beautiful."

Randy's facial expression didn't change. He just

kept staring at the young woman who was speaking to him. After a few seconds, he made a small gesture for Olivia to enter the workroom.

Randy's mother and Olivia exchanged a quick look, and the older woman nodded and led Olivia into the back room. "He rarely invites anyone to his work area."

Sheets of different colored leather and various tools were spread over several tables in the space. Small leather scraps were scattered over the wood floor. A big window looked out over one of the streets next to Fenway Park. It wasn't a game day so the sidewalks were quiet.

A boot, in the process of being made, lay in the middle of Randy's work table. A vine of green and brown leaves started at the ankle of the boot and wound its way to the top of the caramel-colored leather.

As Olivia complimented the young man on his craft, she noticed several pages of sketches to the side of the table. "You're an excellent artist."

Randy sat down on his stool next to his desk. He didn't take his eyes off Olivia.

"How do you communicate with your son?" Olivia questioned.

"Randy understands everything he hears and

reads. Sometimes he makes some sounds, says a few words, but that is rare. He gestures. Once in a while, he draws to communicate. He has a communication book that he uses, it has phrases, words, pictures, sentences. He tried an electronic version of the book, but he didn't like it. He points to what he wants to tell me."

Olivia glanced out the window. "You must love working at your desk and having the baseball park right outside. Can you hear the game while you're working?"

Randy gave the slightest of nods.

"I love baseball," Olivia grinned. "I wish I worked in this room."

Randy reached for a drawing he'd made of one of the baseball players and placed it next to the boot he was creating.

"That's the player he's making the boots for," the woman said.

Olivia walked over to the table to see what Randy had drawn. "Really? He's your customer? I saw him make a great play in left field the night before last. You met him?"

Again, Randy gave the littlest of nods.

"I'm jealous," Olivia smiled.

After seeing several other pairs of boots in

different stages of development, Paulina led Olivia back to the front room of the store with Randy shuffling a couple of yards behind them.

Olivia asked Paulina, "Do you know who delivered the box to Abigail Millett yesterday? Do you have any records of which delivery service might have gone to Ms. Millett's townhouse?"

Paulina looked slightly uncomfortable and she seemed to be toying with a decision. Finally, she let out a sigh. "Randy does some of our deliveries when deadlines aren't looming. It's good for him to get out into the community and maneuver around the city, take a cab, manage communication with strangers by using his book. Randy delivered several packages in the Beacon Hill area yesterday."

Olivia made eye contact with Randy.

"Did you see Ms. Millett?" Olivia asked the man. "Did you leave a box at her townhouse?"

The muscles in Randy's face tensed as his eyes bore into Olivia's, then he turned abruptly and walked away into the back workroom.

Olivia could see his hands were clenched into fists. "Did Randy say anything to you when he returned from his deliveries?" she asked Paulina.

The woman shook her head. "He went straight into his workroom."

"Did he seem upset, was he acting different in any way?" Olivia asked.

"Sometimes, being out in the community makes Randy grumpy and he comes back sullen. That's what he was like yesterday. It wasn't out of the ordinary." Paulina turned to Olivia. "What happened at the townhouse?"

"You haven't seen the news?" Olivia asked.

"We don't watch the news. It's upsetting to Randy. Too many distressing stories so we keep the television off. I read the online Boston newspaper, but I haven't looked at it today." The older woman's face clouded. "What happened? What went on at the brownstone?"

Olivia swallowed hard. "A woman was killed, Abigail Millet. I went to the townhouse to find my friend." The scene popped into her mind and she shivered as her core went cold. "The townhouse's door was slightly open. There was blood on the foyer floor. A box from your store was on the floor near the door."

Paulina's hand flew to her throat. "Someone killed the woman?"

Olivia gave a nod.

"Why?"

"I don't know why."

"Who was she?"

Again, Olivia gave a shrug of not knowing. "I only know her name, nothing else about her."

Paulina's gaze shot to the entryway of the workroom.

"Do you think Randy might have seen something when he was there? Heard something?" Olivia asked.

Paulina's lower lip quivered. "I think he would have indicated to me that something was wrong, that something out of the ordinary, out of the expected routine had happened."

"You didn't notice anything unusual in his behavior when Randy returned?"

"I had two customers here. I was busy with them. Randy came in and went right into the workroom." Paulina's hand rubbed the side of her face. "I can ask him. Will you wait here while I speak with him? He won't be forthcoming if you're in the room."

Olivia nodded. "I'll wait right here."

When Paulina hurried into the work area, Olivia moved quietly to stand near the doorframe, out of view. She could hear Paulina approach her son and speak to him in a soft voice. Olivia couldn't make out the words. She heard scuffling sounds like tools being moved over the wooden desktop. Something hit the floor with a thud.

Paulina's footsteps tapped against the workroom floor and Olivia backed away from the door. The woman's face was tense.

"Randy won't answer my questions. He got angry. It doesn't mean he saw anything. This isn't unusual behavior from him." Paulina crossed her arms over her chest. "I'm sorry. If he indicates he saw anything at that townhouse, I'll let you know." The woman's eyes widened. "I should get in touch with the police if Randy reveals any information. Can I take your number, just in case?"

Olivia told Paulina how to reach her, thanked the woman for her time, and left the shop.

Walking past the leather shop windows on the way to Boylston Street, Olivia stopped in her tracks.

Randy stood at the window of his work room staring out at her. His face was expressionless, but his eyes were somber and sad. He held Olivia's gaze for several seconds, then his shoulders slumped, and he moved away from the window to sit down on his stool where he hunched over his work table and picked up a tool.

5

The morning sun warmed Olivia's face as she walked up the steps of the Alexandria hotel. With a nod, a bellman opened the glass, wood, and brass door so that she could enter the elegant lobby. She checked in and headed for the elevator as her eyes, looking for someone familiar, moved over the people gathered in the glass-walled, high-ceilinged lobby. When would Ynes contact her?

Businesspeople sat at several dark wooden desks tapping at their laptops. A few men and women sat on the sofas and chairs reading newspapers or looking at open leather folders, all dressed in suits or dresses with blazers.

Olivia didn't see her friend among the people so she turned to the banks of elevators to go up to her room. Suddenly, she wheeled around and stared across the lobby at a young woman sitting with a laptop on her legs. The woman's hair was blond, cut short, and she wore tortoise-shell eyeglasses, a black turtle-neck sweater, and black slacks.

Olivia strode across the lobby and as she went, the blond raised her chin a little and took a quick glance at the person walking in her direction.

The blond shut the laptop, slipped it into a leather case, and stood. Making brief eye contact with Olivia and giving her a nod, she left the hotel through the front doors, moved down the granite steps with purpose, and turned left on the sidewalk.

Olivia followed at a distance being sure not to lose sight of her friend. After several blocks, Ynes went into a small café and walked to the rear of the place where she took a seat at a booth.

A few minutes later, Olivia slipped into the booth opposite the woman and with a warm smile said, "I knew it was you. Blond hair, huh? It's a pretty good look."

"Only if it keeps me anonymous."

The smile disappeared from Olivia's face.

Ynes reached across the table for Olivia's hand, and a half-smile moved over her face. "Thanks for coming, friend."

"You have a lot of explaining to do," Olivia said.

"I will. I'll explain everything." Ynes nodded. "But, first, I'm going to tell you a story."

~

THE WAITER BROUGHT food and drinks to the table and Ynes began her tale.

"Do you know the Helena Pruitt Cooper Museum in Boston?"

"Sure," Olivia took a swallow of her tea.

"Have you ever heard of the art heist that took place there?"

"Of course." Olivia covered her scone with clotted cream and raspberry jam.

"That's why I asked you here."

With her eyes wide and her mouth open, Olivia blinked at her friend. "We were only four or five years old when that happened. What does stolen art have to do with you?"

"My mother worked at the Cooper as a security guard. She was working on the night the thieves broke in and stole those paintings ... a dozen paintings worth over four hundred million dollars."

A wave of anxiety rolled through Olivia's stomach. Was Ynes's mother involved in stealing the art? "Was your mother...?"

"No, she wasn't in on it. Nothing could be further from the truth." Ynes pushed her plate away and leaned her arms on the table. "Although, law enforcement did investigate to see if she was connected to the robbers."

"She was cleared of suspicion?"

"She was. My mother worked the night shift at the museum so she could be at home with me during the day. She only worked part-time because she was studying to be a lawyer. My mother loved art, she got her bachelor's degree in art history. She loved to draw, paint." With a sigh, Ynes looked down at her hands and said softly, "That night changed everything."

ELLA CLINTON COHEN, her long black hair pulled into a ponytail that flowed down the back of her uniform, sat at the security desk checking the museum monitors. She glanced down at the small snapshot of her daughter, Ynes, which was taped to the side of one of the monitors near the panic button on the desk, that when hit, would alert the police to a security emergency. Ynes had a slight fever when Ella had left her for the evening shift and she worried that it might have worsened. She would call home in an hour during her break.

Checking her watch, she tapped her finger on the desk. Twenty-seven-year-old Ella was scheduled to walk the west side of the museum galleries, but the second security guard, Tim Mack, was making the rounds of the east side of the museum and had not yet returned to sit at the desk so she could take her turn. Twenty-nine-years old, Tim Mack could be difficult. The man didn't take his responsibilities seriously and he complained endlessly about the low pay and the needed upgrades to the museum security. He often dozed off when he sat at the desk watching the monitors. He sometimes came to work high or drunk. Ella was always on edge when she worked the late shift with the young man, never knowing what to expect when he arrived.

Suddenly, the fire alarm box situated on the opposite wall from the security desk went off, lights flashing and sirens blaring.

Ella jumped to her feet, but did not leave her post at the desk. Leaving the security desk was a breach of protocol. She hit the button on the walkie-talkie and yelled into it. "Where are you?"

"What the hell is going on?" Tim shouted into his hand-held device.

"All the alarms are going off," Ella told him. "Every light is flashing." The fire-security alarm system could pinpoint forty places in the museum where a fire had broken out, or a window had been broken, or a door opened. The system was flashing all forty places at once. "Get back here."

In less than four minutes, Tim Mack ran into the space on the first floor where the security desk was located.

"What the hell?" The man turned off the alarm box, reset it, and turned it back on. All the lights flashed and the alarms started up again. Tim turned the box off. "We'll leave it off for the rest of our shift."

"We need to call the supervisor," Ella said.

"Don't bother. That loser won't come all the way down here in the middle of the night. He never does. We'll leave a note. They can call for a repairman in the morning," Tim said.

"I don't know," Ella looked down at the phone on the desk. "We should report it."

"I've been working here for ten years. They never do anything in the middle of the night. We'll report it by leaving the note." Tim pulled on his earlobe as he walked over to the desk. "That thing nearly deafened me." The young man plopped down in the chair. "Your turn to patrol."

Ella had the urge to place the call to the supervisor anyway, but decided against it since Tim had seniority and she didn't want to get on his bad side. Picking up the heavy flashlight, she started on her rounds to check the galleries, doors, and windows.

Ella loved the artwork in the west side galleries and as she passed her favorites, she admired the paintings hanging in shadow on the dark walls feeling like she was among old friends.

It took just over an hour for Ella to make her rounds. When she approached the low-lit first floor security area through one of the lower galleries, she heard voices near the desk and halted, standing stock still, her heart racing. She edged forward on tip-toes to the doorway and pressed her back against the wall to listen.

"We're here about the disruption." Two police officers stood with their backs to the gallery talking to Tim.

Ella's mind raced. *How did they get in here? Did Tim let them inside the museum? That was a breach of policy.*

"You mean the fire alarms?" Tim asked, a tone of

confusion in his voice. The alarms did not automatically send a notification to the police or fire departments.

"Are you here alone?" one officer asked.

"No. There's another guard doing the rounds," Tim said.

"Call him. Get him down here."

"Why?" Tom asked. "Is something wrong?"

Ella's intuition flashed in her chest. Something about the police officers and their exchange with Tim seemed wrong. She flicked the *off* button on the walkie-talkie in her hand so the thing wouldn't squawk and give away her position if Tim did call her.

"Just call the other guard and get him down here." The officer's voice was gruff.

Ella could hear Tim fumble with his walkie-talkie. "The other guard must have turned it off. There's no signal. I can't contact her."

"Step out from behind the desk," the other officer ordered.

"Why?" Tim's voice sounded feeble with worry.

"Because I said so."

"I'm not supposed to leave the desk."

"Put your hands up where I can see them."

"What? Why? What are you doing?" Tim

sounded close to tears. "I haven't done anything wrong."

Ella's heart pounded so hard she was sure it would break through her ribs. Was the officer drawing his gun on Tim? There must be a mistake. She stepped out of the gallery into the room.

The officers turned to her. One held his gun in his hand.

Despite the adrenaline racing through her veins, she managed to keep her voice steady. "I'm Ella Cohen, the night watchman. What seems to be the problem, officers?" She started walking slowly towards the security desk.

"Hold it, right there."

"How did you gain entry?" Ella asked the men calmly.

"Your pal here buzzed us in."

Ella stopped. She knew these weren't real police officers. She cursed herself for stepping out of the gallery. Making eye contact with Tim, Ella tried to send him a silent message.

Press the panic button on the desk, Tim.

Tim looked pale, wild-eyed, and panic-stricken.

"I told you to come out from behind that desk." One of the officers brandished his weapon.

Like a madman, Tim bolted from behind the desk and raced towards Ella.

The fake officer shot a bullet into the young man's leg. Tim screamed, lost his balance, and hurtled into his partner, knocking her to the ground.

Ella rolled over to see the man dressed as a police officer standing over her, leveling his gun at her chest.

A blinding flash and a deafening roar ... and for Ella Clinton Cohen, everything went black.

6

"Your mother was killed?" Olivia asked gently.

Ynes nodded, her eyes glistening with tears. She reached for her coffee mug and took a long swallow.

"I'm so sorry. I never realized," Olivia said. "Those two men got away?"

"Yes." The pain in the word Ynes uttered tore at Olivia's heart.

"Those are the men who stole the paintings? They were never caught, were they?"

"They weren't caught."

"What about the other guard, Tim Mack?" Olivia asked.

Ynes straightened in her seat trying to collect

herself. "He survived the attack. He's living outside of Alexandria," Ynes said.

Olivia searched her friend's face. "Are you trying to find the stolen paintings?"

"That would be a bonus."

"Why did you bring me here?" Olivia questioned, although she thought she knew what the answer would be. "What do you need help with?"

Ynes bit her lower lip. "I want to find the man who murdered my mother."

A flash of apprehension raced through Olivia's body and she held the young woman's eyes with her own. "What are you going to do if you find him?"

"What would you do in my position?" Ynes looked away for a moment, and then turned back to face Olivia. "*You* killed the man who murdered your aunt."

Olivia winced and all the air in her lungs rushed out. Two years ago, a man killed her Aunt Aggie and while Olivia spent that summer trying to figure out what happened, she got in the killer's way, he abducted her, and tried to kill her. "That was self-defense. He attacked me. He wanted me dead."

Ynes looked contrite. "I know. I'm sorry. My question didn't come out the way I intended. But," she said slowly, "if someone kills another person, does that killer have the right to live? After taking a life?"

Olivia was about to reply, but Ynes spoke first. "Are you sorry that man is dead? Are you sorry the man who murdered your aunt was killed?"

"No." The word that came from Olivia's throat was barely audible. "But, it isn't our place to decide such things. We aren't vigilantes. I won't help you look into the heist if the goal is to kill the man who broke into the museum and shot your mother."

"Will you help me find him if I turn him over to the police?" Ynes asked.

"Will you be able to do that? Will you turn him over to the authorities if you find him? Honestly? Will you give him to the police without harming him?"

Ynes wrestled with a barrage of different emotions and then she said, "Yes."

Olivia nodded. "Abigail Millett from Beacon Hill is not your aunt, is she?"

Ynes seemed to shrink. "No."

"You know what happened to her?"

"I know she's dead. I saw the news." Ynes's brown eyes seemed to darken and her lip quivered.

"Who was she?" Olivia asked.

"I've been searching for my mother's killer since I

was a senior in college. Once, when you and I were at school together I told you I don't trust many people. Abigail Millett was someone I trusted. She had been searching for the paintings from the Cooper Museum heist for years. Abigail had been a professor of art history at Yale for ten years. She left to study for a law degree in order to work in the legal area of art and art history. I met her as I was beginning my search for my mother's shooter. Once in a while, when she found something of interest, Abigail would send me information that she hoped would eventually lead to the identity of my mother's killer."

"Did Ms. Millett die because of her sleuthing?" Olivia asked.

"My guess is she got close to something that someone didn't want her to know. Over the years, she'd made contact with a number of *gangsters*, *criminals*, for lack of better words. She was writing a book about the break-in at the Cooper. She wanted nothing more than to have the paintings returned to the museum. A number of times, she thought she was near a breakthrough ... she was sure she was close to finding several of the stolen pieces. Maybe in her investigating, she learned something that got her killed."

"Why did you tell me she was your aunt?"

"If something happened to me, I wanted you to go see Abigail. I wanted her to know if anything strange happened to me."

"Someone broke into my hotel room in Boston," Olivia said. "The room was trashed."

A look of horror washed over Ynes's face.

"A man who said his name was Michael White came to the hotel in Boston asking for you," Olivia said. "He told us he was your friend."

Ynes sat up straight. "I don't know anyone with that name."

"I knew he wasn't your friend. He said he was there to collect your suitcase."

Ynes's eyes went wide. "You didn't give it to him, did you?"

"Of course not. Brad took it back to Maine. He'll keep it safe."

"There wasn't anything too important in the suitcase. There were some USB drives, but they didn't have anything on them. I wouldn't leave my research files in an unsecured place."

Olivia described what the man at the hotel looked like.

"I don't recognize the description. Who broke into your hotel room? Who was that man who wanted my bag?" Ynes glanced around the restaurant, clearly rattled by her friend's story of the man who had come looking for her.

"Are you in danger?" Olivia asked.

Ynes sighed. "For the past month, I've sometimes felt that I'm being followed ... or observed." She paused.

Olivia said, "We opened your suitcase. We found the *things*."

"It's important to be able to travel without alerting certain people to my comings and goings so I used the two passports. Whoever killed Abigail must know I'm searching for my mother's killer. I believe the people responsible for the heist and the death of my mother will do whatever is necessary to keep their secrets hidden."

Olivia gestured towards Ynes's hair. "That's the reason for the short blond hair?"

"It's a wig. I have some other wigs, too ... shoulder-length auburn hair, chin-length brown hair. Colored contact lenses, different eyeglasses, temporary tattoos. Everything makes it more difficult to identify me. I've gathered tons of information. It's all on those flash drives you found in my suitcase. I feel like I'm getting close."

"Why now? Why have you decided to look for your mother's killer now?" Olivia asked.

Ynes blew out a long breath. "I turned twenty-two at the beginning of my senior year of college. My mother was twenty-two when she had me. She died when she was twenty-seven. The unfairness of it all hit me hard. I started reading anything I could get my hands on about the heist. I started talking to people about it. Why did those robbers have to kill her? Couldn't they have stolen the paintings and let her live? Why did the man who killed my mother get to live?" Ynes looked down at her plate and blinked. "I only remember little things about my mother. Little snippets of life with her. I look at pictures of us together. I think about all the things we both missed." A tear dropped onto the tabletop and the young woman brushed at her eyes.

Olivia leaned forward. "Is it worth it? All this torment? To put yourself in such danger?" She kept her voice soft. "Your mother is gone. It doesn't matter to her. I didn't know your mom, but my bet is she'd want you safe ... happy ... living your life. Maybe it's best to stay away from this, leave it alone. These people don't value anything except a dollar bill. They don't care who they kill, what they steal, who they hurt. If you were my daughter, I wouldn't want you to do this."

Ynes's jaw muscle tensed. "I have to do it, Liv. I have to."

"Why? Revenge will eat you up and spit you out into little pieces."

"It isn't revenge."

Olivia tilted her head. "What is it then?"

"Justice."

The two sat in silence for a few minutes. Olivia worried that her friend had become obsessed with the nearly twenty-year-old crime and was taking chances that would end up getting her killed.

"Have you seen your dad lately?" Olivia asked.

"You mean my *stepfather*. Charles. I never call him *Dad*." Ynes's eyes flashed. "Why are you asking about him?"

"Does he know you've been investigating the heist?"

"He knows of my interest in finding the killer. He doesn't know how much of my time it takes up."

"Would he approve?"

"I don't need to answer that. You know he wouldn't."

"What about your brother? Does he know about your sleuthing?"

Ynes's eyes narrowed. "My *stepbrother* is too busy making money to be concerned with what I do."

Ynes's mother had married Charles Cohen when her little girl was two-years-old. Cohen was twenty-five-years older than Ella Rodriquez Clinton and he had a son, Erik, from a former wife. Now in his early seventies, Cohen, a businessman, investor, and founder of an investment management firm, was a multimillionaire.

When her mother died, Ynes continued to live with Cohen and his son, but she confided in Olivia that she'd felt unwanted and like an outsider. Ynes went off to boarding school at the age of eleven and returned home for summers and holidays. Needless to say, her relationships with her stepfather and stepbrother were not exactly warm ones.

"Can you stay with me for a while?" Ynes asked. "Maybe for two weeks? I have two weeks off before I have to go back to school."

"That depends on what you have in mind." Olivia smiled. "How can I help you?"

"Abigail Millett heard from her contacts that things were heating up about the Cooper artwork. There are rumors that negotiations are going on to return the art to the museum."

"Authorities know where the paintings are?" Olivia asked.

"No, they don't, but noises are being made that the people responsible for the heist want to discuss terms for the return of the art. Abigail told me the crime world was buzzing over it, tempers were flaring, scapegoats were being decided. New information is bubbling up."

"What do you want me to do?" Olivia asked.

"First, I'd like you to interview Tim Mack, the museum guard. He lives about thirty minutes from here. He knows who I am. I talked with him about six months ago. He was defensive about my questioning. If you approach him by telling him you're writing an article on the museum heist since it's soon to be the twentieth anniversary, he might be more forthcoming with information. You'd have to speak with him on your own ... if I'm with you, Mack will clam up."

"What do you want me to ask him? You want him to tell me what happened that night?"

Ynes gave a nod. "I've read his account of the night. I'd like you to hear what he has to say about it. I'd be interested to know if Mack recognized the intruders. Some things he's said in past accounts makes me suspicious about his denial that he did not know the men. Maybe you could get to the bottom of it. I'd also like to know how he managed to survive the attack. Is it possible the robbers arranged the heist with Mack? Did he know them? Did he know the break-in was coming? Did Mack survive because the robbers were careful about where they shot him?"

"You think he'd talk to me? If he feels his answers would place him in a bad light, he might refuse to be interviewed."

"Be positive with him. Take his side. Empathize with him. Don't be challenging. Chat with him. I think he'll respond to you," Ynes said. "He lives in a rundown cottage. He seems aimless. His sister lives in D.C., that's why he left the Boston area and moved down here. He makes money by giving music lessons. I don't know if you'll learn anything new, but it's worth a shot. I'd like your opinion."

"Okay, I'll talk to him," Olivia said. "*If* he'll talk to me."

7

The sky was a brilliant blue when Olivia got off the bus in the small town where Tim Mack made his home. Walking down a quiet lane lined with small bungalows, Olivia found the white house where Mack lived. A picket fence enclosed the front of the place. The grass needed mowing and despite being crowded with weeds, flowers still bloomed in the informal beds around the fence. Two cats curled up on the stone walkway snoozing in a patch of sunlight.

When Olivia called Tim Mack's number and introduced herself, she was certain the man would hang up on her, but following a long expanse of silence, Mack agreed to let her come to his house for a chat. "I can't talk long though," Mack cautioned.

Opening the rickety gate to the yard, Olivia saw a

man emerge from the house through the chipped, black painted front door. He nodded to Olivia and went to meet her.

Mack was just under six feet tall with a very slim build. His hair was long, hitting just above his shoulders, and it was on the thin, straggly side. The brown color had some gray running through it. Mack wore jeans, a flannel shirt, and a worn gray jacket. Olivia knew he was in his late forties, but his face had not aged well, and he appeared to be at least a decade older than his actual age.

"I'm Olivia Miller. Thanks for meeting me." They exchanged a hand shake.

Mack ran his hand over his hair and led her into the cottage where they entered a small sitting room furnished with a faded sofa and two chairs set by an unused fireplace. The coffee table was scratched and scuffed. The place smelled like smoke.

"Would you like a cup of tea or some water?" Mack asked. His manner seemed almost shy.

Olivia told him tea would be nice so the man left and returned a few minutes later with two mugs of black tea and they took seats opposite one another.

"You're a writer?" Mack asked.

"Not exactly. I'm studying law, but I'm doing an article for my former college newspaper. I used to work for the paper when I was an undergraduate student. Since the anniversary of the heist is coming up, I thought it would make an interesting read. The students at the university where only babies when it happened, some weren't even born yet. I was friends with Ynes Clinton, the daughter of the woman who was killed at the museum. I think it's important to keep the story alive. We never know where or when a small thing can happen that eventually leads to a crime being solved."

Mack had looked tense when he'd met Olivia outside in the garden, but he appeared to be relaxing the more he and the young woman talked.

"So your story isn't going to point a finger at me?" Mack asked.

"I just want to write about the incident, what happened, the surprise of it, information about the paintings. Things like that. It's not my intent or desire to place blame on anybody. Although, I know security systems should have been updated at the museum, I'm not out to blame anyone or malign anyone. I understand that most people were doing the best they could. None of us know what decisions we'd make under budget constraints. No one knows how they'd react in a dangerous situation. I'm not here to judge. I just want to tell the story of the missing paintings."

Mack seemed satisfied. "What do you want to ask? Most everything you need to know about my account has been written up in police reports and in news articles. I've had to speak about it over and over." A weary tone tinged the man's voice.

"Reading about something isn't the same as talking with people who experienced an incident," Olivia said. "I appreciate you meeting with me."

"You're from Boston?"

"I was born there and grew up in Boston and Cambridge. My aunt raised me. Now I live in Maine."

"You're studying law?"

"I finished my first year. I'm taking a break right now. I run an antiques shop that my aunt used to own." During Olivia's first year of law school, she'd been plagued by headaches and exhaustion, symptoms of grief over losing her aunt and of the danger she faced after the confrontation with her aunt's killer. Brad and Joe both agreed that taking a year off from her studies would be in Olivia's best interests.

"Your aunt passed away?" Mack asked.

"Yes." Olivia didn't offer any details about her aunt's cause of death.

"What happened to your parents? Why did your aunt raise you?"

"My parents were killed in a car accident when I was a baby. I was in the car when it happened, but I only had cuts and bruises."

Mack blew out a long breath. "Who can say why one person lives through an experience and another does not?"

Olivia knew Mack was referring to the museum break-in. He had survived, but Ynes's mother had not. With a sigh, she said, "None of us can know the answer to that question."

Mack nodded and looked down at the liquid in his cup.

Olivia could sense the man's regret, but was it simply because someone died during the robbery and he'd lived, or was it because he had something to do with aiding the thieves and his partner dying had not been in the plans?

"Can you tell me about that night?"

Mack squared his shoulders and leaned back against the sofa. "I was a musician. I still am, I teach music and play in a band, but back then, I had ambitions and dreams that I'd make it in rock music. I was in a good band, played guitar, keyboards, sang backup. It seemed like we had a good shot at success.

I worked at the museum for years as a security guard. I was always after the management about the need to make improvements to the security systems. They always said it wasn't in the budget." Mack raised his hands in a helpless gesture. "And we know the result of their scrimping on security. Paintings worth millions and millions of dollars lost. A woman's life lost." He shook his head.

"You and Ella Cohen were the only guards on duty that night?" Olivia asked.

"Yeah. Two people always worked the night shift together. I'd already given my notice. I was tired of the work. I had two weeks left." Mack subconsciously rubbed at his leg. "That night was actually my last day at work. I spent some time in the hospital due to my gunshot wounds and never went back to the museum."

"Was the night pretty routine up until those men arrived?"

"Yeah, it was. We took turns doing the gallery rounds. One of us manned the desk and the other walked through the galleries looking for anything that seemed off, a window broken, footsteps in the hallways, checking that everything was in place in the galleries. We registered our walk-throughs by placing our keys in the lockboxes in each gallery room. It was an electronic way to prove we had done the inspections."

"How long did it take to do a walk-through?" Olivia asked.

"A little over an hour. Then we'd switch off, and the other guard would walk around while I sat at the security desk. It was pretty boring work. Once in a while, an alarm would malfunction or someone would press the bell after hours and ask to be let in."

"What would you do when those things happened?"

"We'd turn off the wacky alarm and leave a note for the morning staff so they could call in someone to repair the thing. If someone asked to be let in at night, we'd inform them that the museum was closed and no one was allowed in and they'd go away."

"Who was allowed in at night?" Olivia questioned.

"The museum manager, the head curator, the head of security."

"What about members of the board of directors?"

"They weren't on the night entry list, so *no*."

"But law enforcement officers and fire fighters were allowed in?"

"There was protocol for that. If police officers rang and asked for entry, the policy was to ask for their names and badge numbers and then we would call police headquarters and ask for confirmation that they were real officers and had been sent to the museum for a legitimate reason."

"Did that happen the night of the robberies?"

Mack bit the inside of his cheek. "It did not."

"What *did* happen?"

"I had returned from my rounds and took over the desk while Ella went to do a walk-through. Those so-called cops rang the bell at the back entrance of the museum and said they were there because of the disturbance. I figured it must be about the alarm system going haywire earlier in the night. The whole alarm panel went off, flashing lights, screaming alarms. It's supposed to go off if there's some breach in one of the galleries. It's supposed to pinpoint the particular gallery that's having an issue. Not this time. It was like the thing completely malfunctioned. I turned it off and reset it. When I turned it back on, it did the same thing ... flashing and blaring so I turned the alarm panel off for the night. Someone could call for repairs in the morning."

"Was that the policy?" Olivia asked. "For a

morning staff member to take care of equipment issues?"

Mack sighed. "No, we were supposed to call the supervisor when something went wrong. We didn't call him that night because whenever we *did* call, he would just say to leave a note for the morning security to call for repairs. It was late at night. I figured why bother him."

"So the fake cops said they were there because of the disturbance. That's the word they used?"

"Yeah. Disturbance."

"How would they have known that the alarms malfunctioned? There wasn't any way the alarms notified the police or fire departments?"

"There were no direct notifications except for the panic button on the security desk. If we hit that, it would send an alarm directly to the police station."

"Did you hit the panic button that night?"

"No." Mack leaned his head back and looked up at the ceiling. "I can't explain why not. It was simply me being overcome by the stress of the moment. I didn't even think of hitting the button. It never occurred to me."

"What happened after the cops asked to be let inside?" Olivia asked.

"I asked for their names. They got angry. They

told me to open the door so they could investigate. They said I was hindering the investigation. I got nervous. I could see them on the monitor. They were dressed in uniforms, had badges, they looked official. They told me I could be charged for obstructing police officers in the line of duty." Mack rubbed his face. "I didn't want to get into trouble so I let them in."

"Did you contact Ella by walkie-talkie to tell her the police were demanding to be let in?"

"No. The cops had me pretty flustered. I wondered if the alarms going off earlier was actually an indication of a real problem somewhere in the museum. Had someone actually broken in? I know people criticize me for letting those guys in, but what would most people do when two police officers are yelling at you to open the doors so they can get in? When they're threatening to arrest you because you're interfering with an investigation? Most people would press the damned button to unlock the door."

"I think you're right," Olivia nodded in agreement. "It's unfair to judge a situation like that when you don't experience it yourself. What happened next?"

"The cops came to the desk. They fired questions at me, asked where my partner was. They were belligerent, arrogant, threatening. I started to panic. They told me to contact the other security guard and get him back down there. I tried to get through with the walkie-talkie, but it wasn't working. Ella must not have turned it on when she started out for the walk-through."

Mack's skin looked pale. The lines in his face seemed to have deepened during the conversation with Olivia. "The cops thought I was lying about the walkie-talkie not working. They screamed at me to come out from behind the desk, to put my hands up." Mack's eyes were wide. He didn't seem to be focusing on anything in the room. His vision saw images from twenty years ago.

"Mr. Mack?" Olivia asked gently.

Mack blinked and turned to look at the young woman across from him. "Ella. Ella came out of the lower gallery." He blinked a few more times and his words caught in his throat. "I.... The cop.... Ella...."

Tears poured out of the man's eyes and rolled down his craggy cheeks.

8

Tim Mack used the back of his hand to rub at his face and he got up from the sofa so quickly that the movement startled Olivia. The man rushed from the room and headed down the hallway to the back of the house leaving Olivia unsure of what to do ... should she wait for him to return or go and try to comfort Mack?

She decided to sit, hoping he would come back. After ten minutes passed, Olivia was about to go find the man when she heard his footsteps returning to the sitting room.

Sitting down hard on the sofa, Mack coughed and took a quick look at Olivia. "Sorry," he muttered.

"No need." She shook her head and her light brown hair moved slightly over her shoulders.

"People criticize me for letting that woman get killed. They blame me."

"They shouldn't. It's easy to look at something from the outside and make judgments. They don't know what they're talking about."

"You don't know what it's like." Mack spoke in a whisper.

"I sort of do."

Mack looked at Olivia quizzically.

"I killed someone about a year and a half ago." Sweat moistened Olivia's palms.

Mack's mouth opened and his eyes bugged.

Olivia told him a condensed version of what had happened when she was abducted by her aunt's killer. "He attacked me. He was going to kill me. I stabbed him. I got some hate mail telling me I didn't have the right to take a life, things like that."

"Would they rather you didn't defend yourself and let that monster kill you?" Mack asked gruffly.

"Some people make judgments ... from a distance," Olivia said. "They don't know what it's like to be in a situation."

Mack made eye contact with the young woman and his voice was kind. "I'm sorry that happened to you."

Olivia gave him a half-smile. "Likewise."

"What else can I tell you?"

"You were shot in the leg?" Olivia asked.

Mack nodded. "In the back, too. I had a collapsed lung, part of a rib was destroyed, lots of blood loss. I was lucky. The guy who shot me must have thought I was dead."

"I didn't know you were shot in two places. I thought you were only shot in the leg."

"That's what the news reports focused on."

"Did either of those fake cops look familiar to you?" Olivia asked.

A defensive look formed over Mack's face. "You mean did I know those two?"

"That's *not* what I mean. I know some people wondered if you were in on the heist. I'm asking you if there was anything about those guys that might have seemed familiar. Anything at all. Maybe one or both of those men came to the museum to case the place, to get a feel for it. They might have attended a special event at the museum one evening. They had to have been in the Cooper Museum more than once to know the layout, what was in the galleries, what security was like. My guess is that they were in there many times."

Mack gave a shrug. "Nothing about them seemed familiar."

"Did the museum have security videos or tapes?"

Mack frowned. "The thieves removed the security tape and left with it when they finished the robbery."

"Could those guys have been *real* police officers?" Olivia asked. "Did they plan the robbery and put on that belligerent act so people would think they weren't cops? Everyone is going on the assumption that the robbers were only pretending to be the police. What if they *were* police officers? They'd know things about the museum security. Maybe they worked special evening events at the museum. They'd be familiar with the city's criminal element and could have made a deal with some gangster or mobster."

Mack's face was serious. "I've thought about that possibility, but I don't know. Those guys had an edge to them. They seemed experienced, almost at ease with the whole thing. Real law enforcement officers wouldn't have tried to kill us. Would they?"

"You're right." Olivia sighed. "Those two men had to have a history of criminal involvement to even attempt a robbery of such scale, never mind pull it off."

"I agree," Mack said. "Those two guys weren't legitimate members of law enforcement."

"Can you think of anyone who might have fed the security information and museum layout to some criminal?"

"No."

"I read some of the news stories about the break-in. Some reports mentioned that you occasionally had friends in the museum during your shift for parties."

Mack bristled. "I admit I let some friends in when I was working. *For parties* is a gross exaggeration. At most, there were five or six of us. My friends brought instruments. We jammed together, had a few beers, talked. There were no wild parties. None. I knew the guys. Some of us had been in school together. They were good people. No criminals or low-lifes."

"The two guys who pulled off that robbery had to be smart," Olivia pointed out.

"Clever," Mack said. "Not necessarily smart."

"Was there anyone among your friends who had financial troubles?"

Mack chuckled. "We all had financial troubles."

Olivia asked, "Was anyone so down or depressed about their lack of money that he might be tempted, if approached by someone, to provide information about the museum security?"

"No. Who would even know to approach any of my friends?"

"One of your buddies could have crossed paths with someone. In a bar. At a sports event. Something could have been overheard. An offer might have been made. Maybe the offer was too good to pass up."

"I don't think so." Mack didn't sound one-hundred-percent sure.

"Is there anything else you can think of to tell me?"

"I don't think so."

Olivia gave the man her contact information. "If anything comes into your mind about the heist, please get in touch."

Mack gave a nod.

"How long have you lived in Virginia?" Olivia asked.

"Too long," Mack muttered.

"Are you looking to make a change?"

"I'm moving back to Boston."

Surprise washed over Olivia's face. "You are?"

"In a few days."

"Why the change?"

"I miss Boston."

"How long have you been here?"

"Twelve years."

"You sold your house already?"

"I rent the house. I never wanted to get tied to staying here."

"Well, maybe I'll see you around the city sometime." Olivia shook with the man. "Thanks for talking to me."

"I was glad to do it."

Mack walked her outside to the curb. "Good luck with your article."

OLIVIA MET Ynes in a park across from the hotel. Ynes wore the blond wig and sunglasses.

"He actually broke down and cried?" Ynes asked. "I can't believe it. I've never read anything about Tim Mack breaking down in an interview before. When I talked to him, his manner was short and resentful. He couldn't get rid of me fast enough."

"Maybe I got him on a good day." Olivia pushed her hands into her jacket pockets and told her friend what Mack had talked about. "He seemed sincerely upset about what happened to your mother, about the whole mess of the thing. He admitted to getting flustered and panicking when the officers were shouting at him. He admitted he'd made mistakes and did not follow protocol, not when the alarm system went haywire and by not contacting the Boston Police about the two officers who were ordering him to let them in."

"In person with me, Mack was defensive. He gave the same impression in interviews I've read about him."

"Maybe he's mellowing," Olivia suggested.

"I can't believe he's moving back to Boston. Why now?"

"Are you suspicious of the move?"

"I think I have to be," Ynes said. "Why would he suddenly move back to Boston?"

"He moved to Virginia suddenly, didn't he? Maybe he does that sort of thing."

"What? Every fifteen or twenty years he gets the urge to move to a different state?" Ynes walked for few minutes without saying anything. "It's soon to be the twentieth anniversary of the heist. Is it simply coincidence Mack is returning to Boston now or does he have a reason?"

"What would the anniversary have to do with him moving back to Boston?"

"That's what I'd like to know. No matter how forthcoming he seemed to be with you today, I don't trust him. I think he's hiding something."

"You think he was in on it?" Olivia asked.

"I've always thought so. I think he knew those men weren't real cops. I don't know what his motivation was for doing it. He lives like he has little money. If he got a payoff for letting the robbers into the museum, he's hiding it well."

"Could there have been a different reason for letting them in that night? A reason that had nothing to do with money?" Olivia speculated.

"Like what?"

"A threat of some kind?"

"You mean the robbers might have threatened him with something if he didn't cooperate?"

"It's possible, isn't it?" Olivia asked. "Or what if he had a desire to hurt the museum's reputation or maybe hurt someone who worked at the museum? He told me he'd given his notice, that he was sick of working there."

"Those are good ideas," Ynes said. "If Mack *was* involved, money may not have been his motive at all."

"What's next?" Olivia asked. "Where do we go from here?"

Ynes smiled. "How about back to Boston?"

"That was a brief visit," Olivia kidded. "I didn't get to see much."

"Maybe we'll be back."

"Do you have any idea what happened to the paintings?" Olivia asked.

Ynes sighed. "They're in a warehouse outside of Boston. They're buried in a basement somewhere in Florida. They've actually left the United States and are now in Scotland. They've been split up and have been distributed to members of a gang that operates in Boston. They've been destroyed."

"Destroyed?" Olivia's heart sank. "Do you think that's what happened?"

"No. Those paintings are worth far too much for some idiot to destroy them. There's also a fifteen-million-dollar reward for their safe return. The statute of limitations has run out ... no one can be charged with or convicted of the heist. There are people who know where those paintings are. They're just biding their time."

"Do you think they'll eventually be found?" Olivia asked.

"In a perfect world, it will be us who finds them."

Olivia raised an eyebrow and gave her friend a skeptical look. "Right."

"I'm going to find out who killed my mother," Ynes said with determination. "And if I can keep that reward money out of the hands of a criminal, you bet I'll do that, too."

9
_____

Back in Boston, Ynes drove the rental car along the Massachusetts Turnpike with Olivia in the passenger seat. It was a brisk October morning with the sky the color of cobalt. The woods on both sides of the highway were ablaze with leaves in different shades of red, orange, and yellow.

"Every autumn, I'm reminded how beautiful this time of year is in New England." Olivia watched the parade of color.

"It's spectacular," Ynes agreed. "I only wish it would last a month longer to make winter shorter. Winter is not my favorite time of year."

"Tell me about this man we're going to see in the hospital."

"Jimmy Faber is in his mid-eighties. He uses a

walker. His health is poor. Faber fell down in his prison cell and they thought he may have broken his hip. Turns out it was only bruised, but they're keeping him in the hospital for a week for some physical therapy."

"Why is he in prison?"

"Federal weapons charges. He's been in and out of prison his whole adult life on drug and gun charges. Faber was a person of interest in the museum heist. He's a bigwig in the criminal underworld. He often blabbed that he knew where the art was and who robbed the museum. The FBI promised him lighter sentences if he would cooperate about the art crime. In order to cooperate, Faber wanted the prison time of a friend reduced. It didn't happen. Faber claims the police and the FBI have continuously charged him with false crimes in order to get him to talk about the stolen art. He now says he doesn't know anything about the heist. A few years ago, he submitted to a polygraph test that indicated he *did* have knowledge of the stolen art. Faber says the test was improperly administered and that's why he failed it."

"Maybe he doesn't know anything," Olivia said.

"There's another thing. The sister of a mob associate told the FBI that her brother had received three pieces of art from the Cooper Museum and that he gave them back to Faber shortly before he died."

"What a tangled web."

Ynes said, "Who knows what this guy knows or is lying about. We'll have a chat with him and see how it goes."

"Faber knows we're coming?"

"He knows. It doesn't mean he'll cooperate. Remember, the man is a practiced liar. We'll take what he says with a grain of salt and then analyze the meeting when we get out of there."

"How did you arrange this meeting?" Olivia asked.

"I have a friend in the FBI. I met him while working in D.C. Faber was told we're private investigators."

THE TWO YOUNG women were escorted to Jimmy Faber's room. A police officer sat outside the hospital room in an old wooden chair.

Sitting in an arm chair by the window, Faber looked like he was about a hundred years old. He was overweight, had leathery skin, a head of white hair, and meaty hands. Olivia wondered if the scowl on the man's face was his permanent expression until he turned his head and saw the two attractive young women walking towards him.

"I wasn't expecting good-looking women." Faber's voice was hoarse from years of smoking.

Introductions were made and Ynes and Olivia sat in folding metal chairs.

Ynes said, "A private person has retained us to investigate the Cooper Museum art robbery."

"Your client must be interested in the reward money," Faber croaked.

"Not at all. Our client doesn't care about the paintings."

Faber's thick white eyebrows scrunched together and he huffed. "Come on."

"That's how it is," Ynes said.

"What's the point of the investigation then?" Faber's light blue eyes bore into Ynes.

"The point is to find out who committed the robbery."

"Why? What does that matter? Statute of limitations."

Ynes said, "There is no statute of limitations for murder."

"Your client wants the names of the robbers

because of the woman who was killed?" Faber scowled.

"Yes."

"Why?" Faber asked.

"My client is the murdered woman's daughter," Ynes lied.

Faber's breath moved slowly in and out alternating between a wheeze and a rasping sound. "I don't know who robbed the place."

"Reports suggest you had possession of at least some of the artwork," Ynes said. "Given back to you by an associate before his passing."

"Lies." Faber batted the air with his paw. "FBI lies."

"Why would they make that up?" Olivia asked.

Faber shifted a little on the seat of the fake leather armchair and turned his gaze on the young woman. "Why does the FBI make anything up?"

"To get people to talk."

"Exactly."

"From what we know, the FBI didn't make that up," Olivia said. "You told people yourself that you had the stolen art."

Faber blew out a breath. "No, I didn't."

"More than one person reported hearing you

claim to have the paintings in your possession," Olivia said carefully.

"I never had any of the paintings. People lie. For lots of reasons."

"You took a polygraph test," Ynes said.

"Yes, I did.

"The polygraph claimed you were not telling the truth when you said you never had the art."

Faber shook his head wearily. "The test was not administered correctly so the results were not valid."

"We don't care if you have or had the art," Olivia told the man. "We want to know who was in the museum that night. We only want to know who killed Ella Clinton Cohen."

"I don't know who did it." Faber's chin stuck out.

"Do you know someone who might know the answer to our question?" Olivia asked gently.

Faber gave a quick shrug. "I have no idea who knows what."

"It's been twenty years," Olivia said. "You've probably lost many associates in that time. You're in your eighties now. You probably don't owe anybody anymore to keep the name of the killer quiet. Ella Clinton Cohen was an innocent person. Why couldn't the robbers have just tied up Ella and Tim Mack? Why did they have to shoot them? Those two guards weren't even armed. Two defenseless people were gunned down unnecessarily. One lost her life. Her daughter was only five-years-old. Why give that murderer protection? You don't owe him anything."

Faber stared at Olivia.

Olivia said, "Ella's daughter lost her mother. Nothing was ever the same for that little girl. She had to grow up without the woman who loved her more than anything in the world. That didn't have to happen. Would it be so awful to give Ella's daughter some peace?"

Ynes brushed at her eyes and swallowed hard.

Faber cleared his throat. "I told you," he said softly, "I don't know nothin."

Olivia took in a long, slow breath, her eyes pinned on the old man across from her. She stood up and walked out of the room.

"PEOPLE LIKE HIM MAKE ME SICK," Olivia practically spat. "People who smash up other people's lives without a moment's thought. People who have zero empathy for anyone else, who only care about money and power and making themselves feel like they're a big deal. Being around them makes me feel like I'm covered in slime."

"I know," Ynes said as the two young women walked to the car. "I've met a good number of people like Faber in my search."

Olivia sighed. "I don't think me helping you with this is going to lead to anything new. You've collected endless documents, you've read a thousand accounts, you've talked to so many people. You've covered all the bases. I'm not going to find anything you don't know."

"That's not true. You've been a help already," Ynes said. "You discovered more details when you talked to Tim Mack, and I'd interviewed him previously and read everything I could about him and the heist. Your conversation with him brought out things I didn't know. Your interaction with him brought up things I hadn't thought of." Ynes stopped and turned to her friend. "Your impressions of people can be different from mine. You make me see things in a different way. Please don't give up, Liv. Please stay and help me with this."

"I'm not going to abandon you." Olivia narrowed her eyes and gave her friend a half-smile. "I haven't seen you for a year. Too bad our get-together to catch up can't be going somewhere fun, like a tropical island or something. It has to be sleuthing again like when we were in college."

Ynes chuckled. "Maybe when all of this is over, I'll take you to Hawaii as a thank-you."

Olivia nodded. "I'm going to hold you to that."

"My memory has never been great, you know," Ynes joked. "I might forget all about my promise of a vacation."

"I thought you might say that." Olivia took her phone out of her pocket and held it up. "That's why I recorded you telling me you'd take me to Hawaii."

Ynes said, "It's against the law to record someone without their knowledge."

Olivia shrugged and smiled. "You'll have to prove to the judge that I didn't inform you I was recording."

"Clever." Ynes poked her friend in the arm. "And that's why I asked you to help me."

"What's next on this wild goose chase?" Olivia teased.

"We have an appointment later today to speak with the Cooper Museum director, Clayton Picard. He's been working at the museum for twenty-one years. It's been his mission to find those paintings and bring them back to their rightful place."

"Have you talked to him before?" Olivia asked.

"Yes. I've asked him to meet with us to give us an update on where things stand."

"What's your impression of him?"

"I'll tell you after our meeting. I don't want to influence your opinion one way or the other."

"Okay," Olivia said. "Let's go."

10

Olivia and Ynes sat in comfortable chairs at a round cherry table in Clayton Picard's office. Picard was in his early fifties, tall and very slender, with dark brown eyes and brown hair speckled with silver. He was dressed in a navy blue fitted suit.

"Thank you for seeing us," Ynes told the museum director.

"I'm happy to meet with you," Picard said. "I'm sorry we still don't have any good answers."

"Are there any updates?" Ynes asked hopefully.

"Unfortunately, none that amount to much." Picard shook his head.

"We talked to Jimmy Faber earlier today," Ynes reported. "He still doesn't know anything."

Picard's shoulders slumped slightly. "Mr. Faber is

not a very good liar. We all know he has some infor-mation. Whether or not that information would lead the investigation in the right direction, who can say?"

"Do you still meet with the FBI about the case?" Olivia asked.

Picard's lips tightened. "I do, along with the head of security and two members of the board. We meet in person every two months for information. We speak by phone if anything of interest comes up."

"When all of this started, do you feel everything that could have been done, was done?" Olivia wanted to get an understanding of how the investi-gation had proceeded.

Picard hesitated and then said, "The FBI took over jurisdiction for the case because it was thought the artwork had been transported over state lines. If you talk to the Boston police and the State Police, they'll tell you something similar to what I'm going to say. Most of the members of the Boston police department grew up in the city, they have contacts with criminals, contacts that the FBI does not have. They were not brought into the investigation. Their expertise was ignored. Same with the State Police. We were told in the early days of the case that if suspects aren't found within the first week, then it will, in all likelihood, take years to solve." Picard leaned his arms on the table. "I'm not blaming the FBI. They've done excellent work. But the Boston Police had eyes and ears on the ground that the FBI agents didn't have. In my opinion, the different law enforcement organizations would have been more successful if they'd joined forces. I think valuable time and information was lost." The man shrugged. "That's how I see it, but I suppose it's easy to look back and make judgments. It's been almost twenty years and with each passing year, my heart breaks even more for our loss."

"I've been going over the new website information," Ynes said. "I think it could be very helpful."

Recently, law enforcement had decided to release more details about the heist to the public in the hopes that amateur sleuths would discover some information that might lead to the recovery of the paintings or to the people responsible.

Picard said, "We thought it was time to make use of the internet and open some of the investigation to crowdsourcing. Information about the crime is put online for the public. The technique often brings in lots of tips and clues and has been used to successfully solve crimes. Soon, twenty years will have passed and we haven't solved this thing. Opening up the information will hopefully pay off. The reward has also been upped."

"You've had some situations that seemed they might lead to the recovery of the art?" Olivia asked. She'd read some of Ynes's documents reporting that twice, the museum came close to locating and securing some of the stolen art.

Picard almost flinched, his disappointment nearly palpable. "Yes, twice. I was sure we were going to recover several of the stolen pieces."

"Can you tell us what happened?" Olivia asked.

"The first time was ten years ago." Picard said. "I received a typed letter from an unknown source. The writing and phrasing was articulate and contained a number of legal terms. It made me think that I was dealing with a lawyer who had probably been hired by someone who had the paintings in order to negotiate their return."

"You believed the letter was legitimate?" Olivia asked.

"I certainly did. The writer asked for a certain amount of money which I thought was appropriate. They demanded a promise that law enforcement would not try to arrest the negotiator nor those being represented. Those were the only demands. We were supposed to place something in a local newspaper, a code located on a certain page, if we agreed to the listed requests. I can't tell you what the code was that we used in the newspaper. There are things like that only the people involved would know and law enforcement needs to keep those things from the public."

"What happened?"

"Unfortunately, along with the letter's demands that the people involved not be arrested, the contents of the letter was not supposed to be shared with the agents on the case, only the supervisor. Well, the information *was* shared and the agents went into overdrive trying to figure out who had sent the letter." Picard's face sagged with disappointment. "Somehow the letter writer found out that the FBI was trying to determine his or her identity in order to make an arrest. A second letter arrived. The writer was extremely upset over the attempts to identify him and stated that he or she was afraid to go forward with the negotiation. The person said he would write again at a later time, either to continue the negotiations or to provide us with some clues on how to advance the investigation on our own. No letter was forthcoming. I cannot describe to you the depths of my despair when no letter arrived. We were so close."

"Did the FBI figure anything out about the letter-writer's identity?" Olivia asked.

"No. Nothing." Picard seemed to be reliving his terrible disappointment.

"You mentioned there was a second time you believed you would get the paintings back?"

Picard gave a slight nod. "A close associate of mine, a very wealthy and well-connected person went to a large family reunion in Italy. By an unusual coincidence, a well-known art theft investigator was also in attendance. The investigator spoke at length with my associate. The man had read everything about our stolen art case and he provided information on who the thieves probably were. He believed the heist was executed by local criminals, not by professionals. He also believed the art would eventually be returned when the robbers needed money for other purposes or when they wanted a favor from the feds."

"Interesting," Olivia said. "So do you have any idea who the local criminals might be?"

"The agents believe they might know."

Olivia exchanged a quick look with Ynes.

"Can you share with us who they might be?" Ynes asked.

"It's an ongoing investigation so even if I knew,

which I don't, I wouldn't be able to tell you the names," Picard said. "The FBI keeps that information close to the vest."

"If they know who the thieves are, why don't they make an arrest?" Olivia asked.

"The statute of limitations. They can't be charged with the crime of robbery."

"But they can be charged with something," Olivia said.

"I believe that's so."

"Then what are they waiting for? Why not bring them in? Make an arrest?"

"Because they, and we, want the paintings. We don't care about punishing local thugs, that's secondary to the situation," Picard said.

"It isn't secondary to me," Ynes said softly. "I hope you get the paintings back, but I want to know who killed my mother. And I want someone to be arrested and charged with her murder."

Picard's face paled. "I'm so sorry. I understand. Of course, you do. I didn't mean the FBI wouldn't arrest someone for murder. The FBI wants to bide their time so they can get both the paintings and the killer."

Olivia asked, "I understand the security tape

from the night of the robbery was taken by the thieves. Is that correct?"

"That's right. They removed the tape and took it with them."

"How do you know the thieves took the tape?"

"It's assumed. The tape was missing. It makes sense the robbers took it."

"What if the security watchman, Tim Mack, took the tape?"

"Tim Mack? He couldn't have taken it," Picard said.

"Why couldn't he have taken the tape?" Olivia asked.

"Tim Mack was shot during the robbery. He was bleeding. He was unconscious."

"But couldn't Mr. Mack have removed the tape *before* the thieves entered the museum? What if he was in on it? He could have taken the tape out as soon as he arrived for work that night."

Picard's face clouded. "I suppose that's true."

"In fact," Olivia continued, "couldn't anyone who worked that day have removed the security tape? It isn't checked on a daily basis, is it? I assume one tape would be removed and another would be put in its place every morning."

"That's correct."

"The tape would only be looked at if there was a concern or a reason to do so?"

"Yes, that's right."

"Who even knows if there was a tape at all? Anyone working that day could have taken the tape out or not inserted one when it was supposed to be done. Anyone working that day should be a suspect," Olivia said.

"That makes sense," Picard said.

"Did the FBI treat all employees who worked the day of the heist like suspects?"

"Everyone was questioned. I have no idea if the FBI suspected any of the employees of being involved. It was never brought up with me."

"You worked that day?" Olivia asked.

"Yes, I did."

"Then the FBI may have suspected you, and that might be why they didn't talk to you about it. You may still be a suspect."

"Me? Well, that would be absurd. I've worked tirelessly to get those paintings returned. Perhaps, the FBI initially suspected everyone who worked that day, but we all must have been eliminated by now."

"Is there a list of everyone who worked that day," Olivia asked.

"I'm sure there is."

"Could you email it to Ynes?"

"I could. It might take me some time to find it," Picard said.

"Do you have any advice for us as Ynes and I do more research into who the killer might be? Can you point us in any specific direction?"

Picard ran his hand over his face. He glanced over at Ynes. "Why don't you talk to the director of security? Peter Nelson. He might have some information he can share with you."

Olivia didn't know why, but something about the case seemed off. Like people knew more than they were willing to talk about. *Why?*

11

———

Olivia and Ynes sat in an office in the Cooper Museum building for a second time that day. Peter Nelson, the director of security for the museum, was across from them at the rectangular table. Nelson was tall and lanky, with a handsome face, light brown hair and blue eyes. Olivia estimated he was in his early fifties.

"I've been here at the museum for twenty-two years. I was assistant director of security at the time of the heist. I've studied and learned quite a lot since that time." The man straightened up. "I've actually learned the most about security from what happened here that night almost twenty years ago." Nelson folded his hands and rested them on the table. "I still have nightmares about it."

"We've read about the old equipment, lack of

updates to the security systems and procedures," Ynes told the man. "It was resistance to spending the money necessary to invest in better security?"

"That was part of it," Nelson said. "Training is a crucial ingredient, however. The staff has to be well-trained and well-treated. Equipment can fail, it can be tampered with. We run mock breaches and attempts at break-ins in order for the staff to role-play an incident. Then we get together and analyze. The staff becomes more practiced and aware of things that might get thrown at them. They get to respond to different scenarios. We've also done training for the staff in self-defense. It gives people a better chance to handle a situation."

"Do you think human error was the main problem?" Ynes asked.

"I hate to label it human error," Nelson said. "Two authority figures arrived and bullied a guard into letting them in. They took advantage of the security person's confusion, his wish to assist the police, the fear that he might be arrested, the thought that a mistake was being made that might cause him harm. No one knows what split-second decision we'd make if we were involved in such an event. Hence, we run mock situations."

"You feel the security guards made mistakes that

night?" Olivia asked.

"Most certainly," Nelson nodded.

Olivia could feel Ynes bristle beside her.

"But it wasn't their fault," Nelson added. "It was our fault for not training them properly."

"How do you really know what happened that night?" Olivia asked. "The security tape was taken by the robbers, correct?"

"The tape was missing so the assumption was the thieves took it with them."

"No tape. So the understanding of the event was based on Tim Mack's report of what happened?" Olivia questioned.

"In part. There were security sensors in each gallery that recorded movement in the rooms that night. It gave us information about the movement in the galleries and the time that movement took place. The FBI went through the recorded information and pieced together a timeline."

"The FBI created a fairly accurate account of where the thieves were and when they were there?"

"That's right."

"And the movement matched up with the galleries that had artwork stolen from them?" Olivia questioned.

"For the most part."

Tilting her head to the side, Olivia asked, "for the most part? Are there discrepancies?"

"Some." Nelson adjusted the cuff of his shirt.

"Can you talk about the discrepancies?" Ynes asked.

"Some early news articles mentioned that one of the galleries was entered before the thieves were in the museum. It was the security walk-throughs by the guards. Two paintings were stolen from that particular gallery, but movement was not registered in that room during the time the thieves were at work."

Olivia straightened. "So the two paintings in that gallery were removed *before* the thieves entered the museum?"

"We don't think so. There was a malfunction of the alarm systems earlier that night. Tim Mack reported that all the alarms went off at the same time. He wasn't able to reset the system and left a note for the morning staff to call a repairman."

"Could the robbers have caused the malfunction prior to entering?" Olivia asked. "To cause confusion and make the guards think the police had arrived because of the alarm?"

"We don't think so. There isn't any evidence of that."

"So you think the motion detectors in that gallery weren't functioning properly that night?" Olivia asked.

"The ones in that particular gallery were not."

"But earlier in the night, those detectors registered the movement of the security guards?" Olivia asked.

"That's right."

"The motion detectors stopped working in that gallery shortly before the thieves arrived?"

"It seems so."

"Could the alarm malfunction have caused the problem with the movement sensors?"

"They're weren't connected, they were two separate systems, so no."

"That seems to be quite a coincidence," Olivia pointed out. "The alarm systems went haywire, and then the movement sensors in one gallery stopped working, and then two thieves got into the museum and made off with hundreds of millions of dollars-worth of art, some from the room where the sensors had conveniently stopped working. The FBI doesn't believe those security devices were tampered with?"

"They don't believe so," Nelson said.

"Really?" Ynes asked.

"There is no evidence that anyone interfered

with the functioning. It simply stopped working."

"How convenient for the thieves," Olivia noted.

"It was only the one gallery where the movement sensors stopped functioning," Nelson said. "If the thieves were behind it, they would have tampered with the sensors in all of the galleries they planned to steal from."

"Maybe there wasn't enough time to do each of the galleries," Ynes said. "Maybe the person in charge of disabling the sensors ran into some sort of a problem and didn't have time to tamper with all of them."

"I suppose that's possible."

"And couldn't someone have manipulated the alarms that night to go off all at once in order to distract the security guards? Maybe someone broke in when the alarms went off."

Nelson asked, "If that happened, why did the two men dress up as police officers and ask to be let in? If someone broke in when the alarms went off, why not just open the door for the two accomplices?"

Olivia's mind raced with possibilities. "Maybe the person who broke in when the alarms went off was a backup plan. If the guard didn't let the two fake officers in, then that person would have unlocked a door or maybe shot the guard."

"I don't know." Nelson shook his head. "The FBI has discounted the possibility that more than the two thieves were involved. There was no indication of another accomplice."

"But the FBI holds to the idea that both the alarm system and the motion detector in one of the galleries broke down within an hour or two of each other?" Olivia asked.

"That's right."

"When repair workers came to fix the systems, did they explain why both things broke down?" Ynes asked.

"I don't think they gave a detailed reason," Nelson said. "I believe they mentioned an electrical glitch being the cause. I'm not an electrician and I know nothing about how electrical systems work."

"We've heard the FBI has a pretty good idea of who was behind the crime, who the masterminds were," Olivia said. "What about the two guys who pretended to be police officers? Are their identities known?"

"I don't know."

"What about security tape of the outside of the building?" Olivia asked. "Could you see a car or cars arriving around the museum late that night?"

"The security tape showing the outside of the

building was taken the night of the heist," Nelson told them.

"What about witnesses? Did anyone see a car arrive that night?" Ynes asked.

"There weren't any witnesses."

"What about security tape from the night *before* the robbery?" Olivia asked. "Did that tape show cars driving around the building late at night or suspicious people lurking around the building?"

Nelson let out a sigh. "That tape was missing as well."

Olivia's eyes widened. "The tape from the night before the robbery was missing, too? Did the robbers take that tape?"

"It is assumed that the robbers took the security tapes from the night of the heist and the night before the heist," Nelson said.

"Why did they?" Olivia asked. "Did they do a dry run the night before? Was someone actually inside the museum the night before?"

"Without the tapes, we can't say for sure."

"Did Tim Mack say anything about the night before? Did someone try to break in the night before?" Ynes questioned.

"Mr. Mack claimed nothing of the sort happened, as far as he knew."

"Why would the robbers take both tapes?" Olivia asked. "Did something go on around the museum that needed to be hidden from authorities? Were the robbers here the night before?"

"It could be that they took both tapes just to be sure they had everything," Nelson said.

"Were the tapes marked with the date and then filed?"

"Yes, they were."

Olivia asked, "Then why take tape from the day before? It would be one more thing for the robbers to carry. Unless they had something to hide from that day?"

"I don't think we'll ever know the answer to that question," Nelson said.

"If they find the people who pulled off the heist," Ynes said pointedly, "then we *will* get answers to these questions. Do you think the crime will be solved one day?"

"I certainly hope it will be and that we are able to display those beloved paintings once again."

Ynes had a different reason for wanting the crime solved ... and if law enforcement couldn't solve it, then she would keep looking for the killer for the rest of her life.

12

Ynes had rented a short-term two-bedroom condo on a tree-lined side street off of St. Botolph Street in the Back Bay area of the city. The place had high ceilings, brick accent walls, and a renovated kitchen with high-end finishes. But, most importantly to Ynes was the back entrance to the place which made it easier to come and go undetected.

"Well, well," Olivia said when she entered the condo pulling her suitcase and looked around. "Not too shabby."

"I need a safe place in a quiet neighborhood with good locks on the doors and windows. This place fit the bill." Ynes led Olivia to her room. "It's close to the subway and is two blocks to a busy part of the city which makes it harder for me to be noticed."

Olivia set her suitcase on the bed and chose her words carefully. "You told me you feel like you've been followed and observed. Is it possible that something may have spooked you or that you might have imagined being followed?"

Ynes sat down on the bed. "I was staying at a hotel here in the city. Someone broke into my room and went through my things. Luckily, I had my IDs, laptop, and my flash drives with me. I think someone wanted to find a notebook or my laptop to see what I'd discovered about the heist. Someone doesn't want me looking into this."

"And *my* hotel room was broken into by someone we assume was looking for your suitcase." Olivia sat down next to her friend. "But how did someone know I had your suitcase? How did that Michael White guy know I had your things?"

Ynes said, "When I checked in at the desk two days before you arrived at the hotel, I told them I was leaving my suitcase, but that the room wouldn't be used until you and Brad arrived later. Maybe Michael White paid the desk staff for information about our arrivals?"

"Was Michael White the one who broke into our rooms?" Olivia asked. "Did you tell anyone the name of the hotel where you had the reservation?"

Ynes's face clouded. "I told Abigail Millett and I told my step-father, but I told them I might give the room to a friend."

"Well, somehow that information got around to other people, too."

"I wish I saw this Michael White guy," Ynes said. "I wonder if I'd recognize him?"

"He had a slight English accent." Olivia's face clouded. "Maybe it was a fake accent to make me think he was a friend of yours from Oxford. I know I'm being distrustful of everything, but it's possible Michael White was hired by someone to ask me about your suitcase. Our interaction was brief. He stormed out of the hotel lobby when I wouldn't give him your bag. I'd bet money that someone hired him to come see me and told him to get away quickly if I became suspicious of him. I don't think the actual person concerned with your interest in the case would show his face. He wouldn't want either one us to be able to recognize or identify him at a later time."

"I didn't think of that. It's a good idea. I bet you're right." Ynes stretched and yawned. "I'm starving and exhausted. Let's make dinner. I went to the market before you got here."

Ynes and Olivia went to the kitchen to work on

their meal. Ynes poured some wine, placed a glass in front of Olivia, and leaned against the counter sipping from hers. "What did you think of our meetings with Clayton Picard and Peter Nelson?"

"I think there have been some mess-ups in handling the case. That's probably not unusual, but, gee. The FBI should not have taken over the case without bringing in police officers who knew the city and had contacts in the neighborhoods. That was a blown opportunity. And what about those alarms going off and the motion sensors in the gallery breaking down? Was an accomplice in the museum *before* those two fake cops showed up? How could the alarms and the sensors malfunction at practically the same time?"

"Was Tim Mack in on it?" Ynes asked. "Did he tamper with the alarms and motion detector? Were those things done by him to make him seem innocent? So he could say the security system went crazy that night? So it didn't look like he had a connection to the robbers?"

"And why did the thieves take the security tape from both the night of the heist *and* from the night prior to the robbery?" Olivia asked. "The previous night's tape was dated and filed. The robbers had to have taken the time to look for that tape. Why did they do it? Did something happen the night before? Were the robbers protecting someone? Did someone let the thieves in the night before so they could do a dry run?"

"If that was the case, someone in the museum was in on the heist," Ynes said.

"It wasn't necessarily Tim Mack. Any staff member could have been working late. On purpose ... so they would be able to help the thieves get in or could help them with the actual theft."

"The FBI claims to know who was behind the heist," Ynes said.

"Does that mean the mastermind or the robbers?"

"I think it means the mastermind. If they knew who was in charge of the heist, why don't they arrest him?" Ynes asked.

"Like the director said, the statute of limitations," Olivia said. "The mastermind can't be charged with the crime of stealing the paintings. The time for prosecuting the theft is up. Maybe the FBI is working with the mastermind to find out the names of the actual robbers ... and the name of the person who killed your mother. There is no statute of limitations on murder. The FBI also wants to recover the paintings. There's no good reason to arrest the mastermind. Maybe the person wants something in return ... like the release of a friend from prison. Maybe those details are difficult to work out."

Olivia plated the dinner and they carried their meals to the dining area of the living room. "You told me you have a friend in the FBI. Did you ask him if the department knows who killed your mother?"

"He couldn't tell me that. He doesn't know a lot about the details of the case. He's based in D.C. and doesn't have a lot of close contacts up here. He's able to help sometimes with things like getting me in to talk to that mobster in the hospital."

"Have you found some criminals to talk to besides the sleazy guy we met in the hospital?"

"A few low-level types. People who were once involved with the Boston crime circuit, but got out of it years ago. They're careful about what they say. They don't trust me. They don't want to get into trouble. I didn't learn much of anything." Ynes placed her fork on her plate. "But ... money has a way of greasing the rails."

Olivia tilted her head and looked at her friend. "Meaning?"

"I have a trust fund. My stepfather set it up after my mother died. It was a stipulation she had put into the prenuptial agreement. She wanted to be sure that if anything happened to her, that I would be provided for. I've recently been given the proceeds of the fund." Ynes took in a long breath. "Money talks. Maybe I can use my new-found wealth to get some people to talk."

Olivia raised an eyebrow. "It certainly won't hurt. How will you find people who are involved with the criminal side of the city?"

Ynes put her chin in her hand and leaned on the table. "That's yet to be determined."

"I've been thinking. Did your mother have a close friend in the city? Someone she may have confided in, maybe told some things that she was worried about."

Ynes blinked. "Yes. She had two good friends. You think we should talk to them?"

"Why not? Maybe they know something or suspect something. Are they still living in the area?"

Ynes nodded. "They email me every now and then to see how I am. They used to visit me when I was younger. I could contact them and see if we could meet."

"I think it could be helpful," Olivia said. "Someone from the past, someone who knew your mother well. It might lead to nothing at all, but who knows? One little thing can lead to a different little thing, and then to another."

Ynes asked, "Do you have any other ideas about who we should talk to?"

Olivia didn't answer right away, but then said, "You might not like suggestion."

Narrowing her eyes, Ynes asked, "Who is it?"

"Your stepfather."

Ynes pressed herself back against her chair and stared at Olivia. "Why him?"

"He's a very wealthy man. He has contacts in the city. I bet he knows a lot of things that go on ... a lot of things that went on."

"No," Ynes said.

Olivia blew out a breath. "Why not?"

"I don't want him knowing that I'm looking into this."

"But, why not?"

Ynes looked down at the table. "I don't know. I don't want his help."

Olivia spoke slowly. "You want to find out the answer to your question ... who took your mother's life? Who cares who helps you arrive at the answer?"

With her hands clenched tightly together, Ynes nodded and lifted her eyes to her friend. "Okay. I'll call him and arrange a time when we can meet."

13

_____

Cassandra Lark was in her late forties, tall and slender with graceful movements that hinted at training in dance. Her chin-length blond hair was cut in layers around her face and her blue eyes were sharp and intelligent. Wearing a black skirt and a navy blazer, the woman crossed the dining room of the trendy restaurant, wrapped her arms around Ynes, and held her for a long time.

"My gosh." Cassandra stepped back a little still holding Ynes's hands. "You are the image of your mother." She placed a hand over her heart and took a moment to compose herself. "I miss her still."

Ynes smiled and was surprised at the sudden rush of emotion she felt at seeing her mother's dear friend.

Olivia stood near the table watching the warm reunion between the two women.

Ynes introduced her friend and they took seats.

"I was so happy you emailed to meet. It's funny, I was thinking of you just the other day." Cassandra leaned forward. "I can't believe you're working on your master's degree. Where have the years flown off to?"

After general chat and catching up with one another, Ynes said, "We wanted to meet with you to ask about my mother."

Cassandra sat up, surprised. "How can I help?"

"Soon it will be the twentieth anniversary of the heist at the Cooper Museum," Ynes said.

"Twenty years already," Cassandra whispered.

"I've been thinking about my mother. More deeply than I ever have in the past. I barely remember her, but the things I do recall are full of love and fun and feeling cared for. When I turned twenty-two, I realized that was the age my mother was when she had me."

Cassandra smiled warmly at Ynes.

"I was overcome with sadness about all we lost. I decided to look into her murder."

A frown formed over Cassandra's face.

"I want to know who killed her. I want the person brought to justice."

"I understand." The blond woman reached across the table and squeezed Ynes's hand. She said softly, "You were both cheated out of so much."

"Olivia and I thought it might be helpful to talk to you about my mother. We wondered if you can recall back to the days twenty years ago when you were friends and tell us if there was anything my mother seemed worried about or nervous about or anything at all."

Folding her hands together, Cassandra said, "I remember so many things from back then, just like they were yesterday. Ella and I were like sisters. I loved being with her. We were so close, we just clicked." The woman sighed. "I knew her before she met your stepfather. You know about your biological father?"

"I know he was killed in a car accident when my mother was three months pregnant."

"Yes." Cassandra nodded. "Ella was so strong, so determined to give you a good life." She smiled. "I was with her in the hospital when she gave birth to you."

"I didn't know that," Ynes said.

"Your mother absolutely adored you. Her eyes shone with love whenever she looked at you. How she doted on you." Cassandra's face brightened at the thought of Ella with her little daughter. "Your mother met your stepfather, Charles, when you were two. That man was smitten with Ella. He was already a very wealthy man and was years older than your mom. Your mother hesitated at his interest in her, but Charles sent her flowers every day for a month, took her out, called her, sent her cards. The man would not give up and finally your mother agreed to marry him. Six months after they met, they were married."

"Was she happy with Charles?" Ynes asked.

"I would say, yes ... content, anyway. Comfortable. Charles was about twenty-five years older than she was. He ran a company, was often too busy. I think a younger man would have been a better match, but...." Cassandra shrugged. "Your mother insisted on a prenuptial agreement. It was to protect you, should anything happen to her. She wanted a trust fund set up so you would be taken care of financially. She told Charles she wouldn't marry him without it. Charles was happy to do it."

"My mother was studying law when she died," Ynes said.

"She always wanted to be a lawyer," Cassandra said. "She loved the law. Ella did not want to be a woman who depended on her husband. She wanted to make a financial contribution to the family, have work of her own. You know she loved art. When she heard about the opening for a security guard at the Cooper, she jumped at it. She loved that museum. When she finished her studies, she hoped to work as a lawyer for a museum or an art house or in intellectual property protecting artists and artwork."

"Did she like working at the Cooper?" Ynes asked.

"Ella loved being around the art, but she often talked to me about her concerns about security. She didn't think the board of directors took the museum's security seriously. When proposals for updates and upgrades to the security system came up, the board would dismiss the notion that new things were needed or would do something less expensive than what was suggested." Cassandra shook her head. "We know Ella's concerns were valid."

"Did she meet with her supervisors about her concerns?" Olivia asked.

"Oh, yes. She told me they politely listened to her, but nothing was ever done to improve the systems. Your mother became very frustrated."

"What about the other guards?" Olivia asked. "Did Ella mention the people she worked with? Did they support her ideas that security improvements were needed?"

"She did talk about her co-workers. Some just wanted to do the job, collect their pay, and go home. A couple of her colleagues wanted improvements and pressed for them. The man on duty with her the night of the heist was especially vocal about what was needed."

"Tim Mack," Ynes said.

"Yes," Cassandra said. "Ella told me that Tim Mack gave up eventually. He'd been pressing for changes for years. That last year, he'd had enough and gave his notice."

"Did my mother get along with Mr. Mack?"

"She did, but he was difficult to work with that last year. Tim didn't care about the job anymore. He told your mother that sometimes, he let friends into the museum late at night and they drank beer and listened to music. Sometimes, his friends brought instruments with them and they played together. Your mother didn't like that. She felt Tim had become too lax. Ella talked to me quite often about her worries about the security issues and about Tim.

She talked it over with your father, too ... asked advice about how to handle it."

"Did she ever mention that Tim might have had a grudge against someone at the Cooper?" Olivia questioned.

"Tim did not like the head of security. Ella told me they bumped heads all the time. I can't recall the man's name. He left the Cooper a few months after the heist."

"Did my mother ever say she was concerned that Tim would do something stupid?" Ynes asked.

"You think Tim might have assisted the thieves?" Cassandra asked.

"I don't know what to think," Ynes said.

"I have to admit I wondered if Tim Mack was in on the heist," Cassandra said.

"Did my mother ever tell you that the security alarms went off for no reason during her shifts?"

Lines formed on Cassandra's forehead as she thought about the question. "I can't remember if she mentioned anything like that happening."

"What about the motion detectors in the galleries?" Olivia asked. "Did Ella ever tell you those weren't working as they should be?"

"Again, I can't remember those details," Cassandra said. "I'm sorry."

"Was my mother suspicious of anyone at the museum? Did she tell you she wondered if anyone was up to no good? Were security tapes messed around with? Did the alarm system have problems that no one fixed? Anything odd like that?"

"I only remember the usual complaints that the systems and protocols should be updated."

"What did she say about protocols? What should be updated? Was she specific?" Olivia asked.

Cassandra said, "Ella thought that there should be four guards on duty for each shift. She thought two people weren't enough. It was a big museum. Ella didn't think two guards were enough to handle a serious situation. She thought the guards should work in pairs so that if anything went awry, the night watchmen could discuss the emergency and come up with a plan together ... not be alone or only in contact with the other guard by walkie-talkie. Ella thought that was important to properly protect the artwork and to increase personal safety for the guards. She was right, wasn't she." A look of alarm washed over Cassandra's face and she looked pointedly at Ynes. "You aren't searching for your mother's killer on your own, are you?"

"Olivia is helping me," Ynes said.

Cassandra's eyes took on a panicked look. "Oh,

no, Ynes. Let the investigators handle it. It's too dangerous. Don't go near the criminals. Your mother would not want you to put yourself in harm's way. Don't risk it. Please. For your mother's sake."

Ynes said softly, "It's for my mother's sake I'm doing it."

14

"You lookin' for something?" a man's voice asked.

Olivia and Ynes stood at the end of an almost empty wharf in Boston's North End looking out at the sparkling lights shining over the harbor. They'd had dinner in one of the small, Italian neighborhood restaurants.

Ynes wore an auburn wig and a pair of eyeglasses despite Olivia's protests that a disguise was unnecessary. "If someone is watching me, I don't want them watching you, too. I'm hard to recognize when I wear a wig and glasses."

The young women turned towards the voice and saw a man in dark clothes standing in shadow. They didn't think he was talking to them so they looked away.

"Did you hear my question?" the voice asked.

Ynes took Olivia's arm and began to steer her away from the water and the man who seemed to be trying to talk to them.

"I know who you are," the man said.

"Are you talking to us?" Olivia asked.

"Don't respond to him," Ynes whispered.

"I know you're the daughter of that woman who died in the museum."

Ynes stopped dead and glared at the man. "What do you want?"

"I asked if you're looking for something." The man took a drag of his cigarette and the end of it glowed orange in the darkness.

"Yes, I'm looking for something. Do you know something?"

"It's possible."

A cool breeze blew off the water and Olivia zipped up her jacket while keeping a close eye on the figure. The man was slender, wiry looking. He had a baseball cap pulled low over his face. Olivia judged him to be in his sixties.

"What can you tell us?" Ynes kept her distance from the man.

"I hear you're interested in the museum heist."

"I'm interested in who killed my mother."

"One and the same," the man said.

"Do you know who pulled off the crime?" Olivia asked.

"I might."

"How do you know who I am?" Ynes questioned.

"Word on the street says you're investigating. I see you around. Lots of people see you around. The wigs don't help, by the way."

Olivia flicked a glance at her friend.

"Why would you help us?" Olivia asked.

"Most of us feel the same way. It's been a long time. Those paintings need to go back. The purpose wasn't fulfilled."

"You understand *our* main purpose is to find out who killed Ella Cohen?" Olivia tried to get a look at the guy's face. "Not to retrieve the artwork."

"I've heard, but you might be able to kill two birds with one stone."

"Why us?" Olivia asked. "There are lots of people trying to figure this out ... law enforcement, journalists, regular citizens. Why don't you talk to them?"

The man threw his butt down on the pavement and ground it out with his heel. "Reasons."

"What do you want in exchange for the information?" Ynes asked, her eyes narrowed.

"Guess."

"Money." Ynes's jaw was tight.

"Good guess, but not this time. This is a freebie."

"Why?"

"Not my call. I'm just the contact. I'll give you an address. You go there tonight at 11pm. Just the two of you. If you reach out to law enforcement or anyone at the museum, the meeting is off. We'll know. Stand out front, by the door. Someone will meet you. Interested?"

"Okay." Ynes gave a nod.

Olivia was pretty sure this was a bad idea, but decided to keep quiet for the time being.

The man told them the address. "Got it? Need anything repeated?"

"We're good."

The man pulled up the collar of his coat and started away. Pausing, he said without looking back, "I hope you get what you're after." Then he disappeared into the darkness.

Olivia faced her friend. "I don't think this is a good idea."

Ynes stayed quiet.

Looking at her phone, Olivia pulled up a map of the address. "It looks like an area of industrial buildings in Quincy. At 11pm? In the dark? Just us? I don't think so."

Ynes looked down at the ground. "I think we should go."

Olivia sighed. "It's a dumb thing to do."

"If I don't take the opportunities that are presented, then I lose a chance to find what I'm looking for. I'll go alone. That way, if you don't hear from me, you can contact the police."

"Right. You're going alone? Absolutely not." Despite the nervous tightening of her stomach, Olivia refused to have Ynes go to the meeting on her own.

"If someone wanted us quiet or felt threatened or wanted us to stop looking into this, that guy could have shot us right here on the wharf and be done with it," Ynes said.

"An uplifting thought." Olivia looked back over her shoulder. "Let's walk back to where more people are around. It's pretty creepy he found us and we didn't notice him at all."

"We should be more observant." Ynes sounded like she was lost in thought and far away.

"We don't have the experience they have," Olivia noted. "Or the network or the contacts."

"That's why someone is reaching out to us," Ynes said. "We're nobodies. We don't have connections to the criminal element. We're on the outside looking in."

"Maybe." Olivia shoved her hands into her pockets. "When we get there, you better be on your toes with that karv-whatever because that's our only defense."

"Krav Maga," Ynes corrected her friend. Ynes was an expert at Krav Maga, a self-defense and fighting system that used techniques from judo, wrestling, karate, boxing, and aikido, and emphasized offensive and defensive movements and maneuvers. A couple of years ago, Ynes used her skills to take down a professional football player who was strangling Olivia behind a nightclub in Boston. "I'll be ready."

After having coffee and sitting for an hour and a half to pass the time until they could go, Ynes used her phone to order a car to pick them up and drive them to the location. Traveling south on I-93, the driver turned off and, following directions from the car's GPS system, drove another fifteen minutes before pulling into an industrial park's lot and stopping in front of a four-story brick and concrete building that had seen better days. The dark lot was deserted. A couple of floodlights shone down from the top of the building.

"You sure this is the place?" The driver peered out the window of the car at the desolate location.

"Yes." Ynes opened the passenger side back door while Olivia leaned forward to speak with the driver.

"I'd like you to wait. Can you pull back behind the building and stay there for a while? If we aren't back in fifteen minutes or so, you can take off." With arrangements made for the car to wait for them, Olivia got out and stood next to Ynes.

"Let's go." Ynes headed for the door to the building and the two women waited in the cold night air for someone to contact them.

Whenever a vehicle made its way down the street, Olivia's chest would clench in anticipation, but each truck or car kept on its way going past the parking lot. "Maybe no one is coming," she said.

"Let's wait a little longer." Ynes's tone was tinged with disappointment. "Why wouldn't someone come?"

"It could be that the person is watching us. Maybe he or she wants to be sure we followed the instructions and didn't contact police or museum staff. Tonight might be a test."

"To see if we're trustworthy?" Ynes asked.

Olivia nodded. "Exactly. If no one comes tonight,

I'll bet you'll be contacted again and then the next meeting will actually take place."

Ynes blew out a long breath and shivered. "It's freezing. Let's wait five more minutes."

"That's all the time we have, otherwise our driver will leave us here."

"We can call another car," Ynes pointed out.

"Yes, but then we'll have to wait in the cold even longer." Olivia stamped her feet to warm them. "It's only October. Why is it so cold?"

Ynes leaned against the building.

"You okay?" Olivia asked.

"Am I going to find the answer about my mother?" Ynes sounded defeated.

Olivia turned to face her friend. "I don't know. I think truth will come out eventually. That guy at the wharf told us some unusual things, *it was time for the paintings to be back where they belong ... it's been too long ... the purpose wasn't fulfilled ... most of us feel the same.* It might be too complicated for us to figure this out. From what I've read, there are too many layers to this case, too many gangsters involved, just too everything. If you find out something that will break the case, it will be by chance, it will be because somebody wants this whole thing to be over and done with."

"Is that what tonight is about?" Ynes asked. "Is someone going to tell us something that other people have been searching for over the past twenty years?"

Olivia gave a shrug. "Or it's a wild goose chase and someone was pulling our legs."

"You think that guy told us to come here as a joke?"

Olivia looked to the dark street. "No, I don't." She squeezed Ynes's arm as a dark sedan pulled slowly into the lot and she could feel her friend stiffen.

The car came to a stop. Olivia could see the rear passenger window slide down. Her heart nearly stopped beating as she waited for what would happen next.

A hand moved up and dropped something onto the concrete. The window went up and the car drove out of the lot and up the street.

"What is it?" Ynes whispered.

"One way to find out." Olivia started moving towards the thing on the ground.

Ynes squinted. "An envelope?"

A small brown envelope. The breeze rustled one corner of it and threatened to lift it into the air.

Ynes picked it up, ran her finger under the seal, and removed a small piece of white paper.

Tobey Sewall was printed on it.

"Do you know anyone by that name?" Olivia asked, looking over Ynes's shoulder.

"No one." Ynes stared at the words. "What does it mean?"

"I have a feeling we'll be finding out," Olivia said.

15

Charles Cohen was tall, broad-shouldered, and trim. His hair was white, his eyes blue, and his skin looked to have a slight tan to it. In his early seventies, Cohen wore a well-fitted dark gray suit with a white shirt and a blue tie. The man's gaze was direct and confidant. Olivia could imagine him leading a board of director's meeting or presenting to a room of stockholders.

Cohen's home was an impressive four-story townhouse in Boston's Back Bay. The place was elegantly decorated and the brownstone would be perfectly suited to a layout and story in a prestigious architectural magazine. Olivia felt like she was in a fancy and much-too-expensive city hotel.

"You live in this place?" Olivia whispered to her friend.

Ynes rolled her eyes. "From time to time."

Cohen was in his study when Ynes and Olivia arrived. He rose from behind his desk with a warm smile and came around to embrace Ynes. "You look wonderful."

Olivia was introduced, they shook hands, and were about to take seats on cream-colored sofas set by a fireplace when Tilly, the housekeeper, rushed in and grasped Ynes in a bear hug.

Tilly kept her hands on Ynes's arms. "Look at you. So beautiful. So much of your mother in your face. I miss you." She hugged the young woman again and then hurried away to get coffee and tea. Tilly, in her early sixties, had been Cohen's house-keeper since before he married Ella. Short and petite, Tilly had silver gray curls cut short around her face, bright blue eyes, and a warm, friendly smile.

Listening to Ynes and her stepfather talk, it was clear to Olivia that they hadn't seen one another for months. There was an odd formality to their conver-sation that made Olivia grateful that she'd had such a warm, loving, and easy relationship with her Aunt Aggie and with her neighbor and almost-dad, Joe.

"You'd like to talk about your mother?" Cohen asked.

Sipping from the delicate tea cup Tilly had brought in, Ynes said, "Yes. The past couple of years, I've been thinking about Mom a lot. The heist haunts me. If she hadn't worked that night, well...." Ynes let her voice trail off, her eyes growing misty.

"I understand," Cohen said. "For years after Ella's death, my thoughts would torment me about what might have been. If only this, if only that. Wallowing in those thoughts was not healthy for me and I had to force myself to go on." Cohen made eye contact with Ynes. "After your mother died, I didn't do anything right. I had no idea how to raise a daughter. With Erik, his mother did everything ... until she died. After my first wife's death, I didn't know how to deal with Erik either."

Cohen ran his hand over his face. "After Ella was killed, I totally immersed myself in the business. I wasn't there for you. I give you my most sincere apologies."

Ynes seemed taken aback, her face turned pale and her eyes went wide. She opened her mouth as if she would say something, then hesitated and closed her lips. "Thank you," was all she managed.

"Erik was a handful. He was a very, very difficult child to raise. He was always getting into trouble at school. He is an intelligent man and has straightened himself out, but years ago, he didn't apply himself. He was wild and acted out. Erik wanted to be a rock star. He got into lots of trouble. Sometimes, he'd sneak out of the house in the middle of the night. Sometimes, the police returned him home." Cohen sighed. "Your mother had a nice way with Erik. I thought she would do him a world of good." The man's eyebrows raised. "Of course, that's not why I married your mother. I loved Ella deeply. But I also believed she would be a good influence on Erik." Cohen clasped his hands in his lap. "Erik had other ideas and kept up his wild behavior. Sometimes, he was disrespectful to Ella, but she always handled the boy with aplomb." Shaking his head, Cohen said, "I'm babbling. When you said you wanted to talk about your mother, my head just flooded with memories. What is it you'd like to know? What can I tell you?"

"Mom worked at the Cooper. She was attending law school. I've been thinking about her life and about what might have been. I want to know more about her. I want to know what happened that night." Ynes didn't mention that she'd already talked to Ella's best friend, Cassandra Lark. "Did Mom express concerns about the security at the Cooper?"

"She did. She often complained that the security system was out of date, that the guards didn't receive enough training, that policies needed to be updated. Your mother told me that some information had come in that some thugs were planning to rob the place. Nothing was done about the rumor, nothing at all. She ... and I ... were appalled that with information like that, the board did nothing to improve security. Ella thought the guards should work in pairs and that four night watchmen should be on duty during every night shift."

"How did she get along with her co-workers?" Ynes asked.

"She got on fine with them. Ella was very professional and took her work seriously. She loved the artwork and felt it her duty to protect it. Some on the staff didn't feel the same way and at times, there were some ruffled feathers and some disagreements, but all-in-all, Ella liked and worked well with the other guards."

"Was there anyone in particular she didn't approve of?"

"One of the guards, Tim Mack. Ella liked the man, but she didn't think he took his job seriously. I guess he'd given his notice and had given up on the work, taking it easy, blowing things off. Your mother said that sort of thing had gone on for a few months."

"Did she ever express concerns about anyone else who worked at the Cooper?" Ynes asked. "Did she have any suspicions, that in retrospect, may have pointed to someone who may have been involved in the heist?"

Cohen shook his head. "I don't remember her saying anything like that. She didn't like the lack of progress on updating the security systems, but there wasn't one person to blame. It was a systemic failure across the board."

"Did you sue the museum after she was killed?"

Cohen looked surprised by the question. "No, I didn't."

"Why not?"

"I didn't need the money. I didn't want to hurt the museum financially. Ella loved the Cooper. It didn't seem right to file a lawsuit against them."

"Did you ever hire anyone to find out who was responsible for my mother's death?"

The man's eyebrows raised. "I didn't. I left it to law enforcement. I had no reason to think a hired private investigator would do a better job than the FBI."

"You have a lot contacts in the city. You know a lot of people. Have you heard anything about why the case is still unsolved?" Ynes asked.

"My understanding is that the incident needed to be handled delicately. The FBI didn't want to set off a gang warfare. When a big crime takes place in a part of the city, the people responsible for doing the crime are supposed to pay a tribute to the gang boss who claims that part of town. I've heard that wasn't done and trouble was brewing between at least two factions. The investigation had to be handled with kid gloves for a while."

"Does the FBI know who stole the paintings? Do they know who killed my mother?"

"They thought they did. Now, I don't think they're so sure."

"Do they know where the paintings are?" Olivia asked.

"No. There have been some hopeful developments over the years, but none have panned out."

"Do you think someone who worked at the Cooper was in on the heist?" Olivia asked.

"I wouldn't be surprised," Cohen said turning to the young woman. "If your next question is, who do I think it was, I can't answer that. I have no idea."

Ynes said, "I've read that the security alarms

malfunctioned that night as well as one of the gallery's motion detectors. Did Mom talk about the alarms malfunctioning as something that happened on a regular basis?"

"She didn't, no."

"Did Mom seem nervous about anything right before she died?" Ynes asked.

Cohen said, "She never reported to me that she was feeling nervous or worried about anything and I didn't pick up on anything like that. Things seemed normal. The usual routine."

"I was only five when my mom was killed. How did Erik handle my mother's death? We rarely interacted."

Cohen's facial muscles tensed. "Erik's mother died when he was seven. I think that contributed to the problems in his behavior. When Ella was killed, Erik went off the deep end. His moods worsened, his bad behavior escalated, he started taking some drugs. He'd only just turned eighteen and he'd lost two women in his life. Things were quite a mess for some time. Erik went off to a camp for troubled young men for a year, working outdoors, learning about the wilderness. I hired a man to look out for him, keep him on the straight and narrow. Then he went off to college and I kept the man on salary to keep Erik in line and make sure he didn't do anything to screw up his life."

"It worked obviously," Ynes said. "Erik has a good life. He's a president in your company. He's successful and respected."

Cohen's expression darkened and his lips tightened. "And I'll make sure he remains so." The man checked the time. "I'm sorry, but I must get to the office. Is there anything else you'd like to ask?"

"I guess not," Ynes said.

"How long will you be in town? Why don't we have dinner?" Cohen suggested.

Ynes told him she'd get in touch.

As she and Olivia were heading out of the office, Ynes asked, "Do you happen to know anyone by the name of Tobey Sewall?"

Olivia watched as something flitted over Cohen's face. It was gone in a second and the man forced a smile. "Who is that?"

"I don't know. I wondered if you'd ever heard the name."

"Where did you hear it?" Cohen asked.

"Just in passing."

"I'm not familiar with the name," Cohen said.

Ynes stepped into the hall and Olivia followed.

Olivia had the distinct feeling Cohen had heard the name.

16

Erik Cohen met his stepsister and Olivia in his Boston office. He stood up from his desk when they came in and greeted Ynes warmly with a long hug. "You look great. Everything going well for you?"

Thirty-eight-year-old Erik looked very much like his father, tall, athletic, broad-shouldered, blue eyes. His sandy hair was cut short and he wore a well-fitted suit.

"Everything's fine," Ynes said. "This is my friend, Olivia Miller."

After introductions, they sat on comfortable sofas that were set near the floor-to-ceiling windows affording a magnificent view over the city and the harbor.

"Dad told me he saw you the other day," Erik said. "He said you had a good talk."

Ynes nodded. "He told you what we talked about?"

"He did." Erik leaned forward in his seat with a concerned expression. "Are you okay?"

"I'm fine."

Erik said, "It's just ... well, it seems the heist and Ella's death are weighing heavily on you."

Ynes's eyes flashed. "I lost my mother ... to violent circumstances. The impact of that loss has recently hit me hard. From what I've read, it is not uncommon for someone who lost a loved one as a child to wrestle with the circumstances and implications when they reach their twenties. That, apparently, is what's happening with me."

"It's understandable." Erik looked warmly at his stepsister. "Is there anything I can do to help?"

"You'd just turned eighteen when my mother died. You had a different perspective than I did as a five-year-old child. I wondered what your relationship was like with my mother."

Erik made a face. "I was a jerk back then. I didn't want Dad running my life. He was always on me to do better in school. I hated it. I rebelled. Ella had a sweet way that made me more amenable to behaving, but her suggestions and advice never stuck with me for very long. The next morning, I'd be back to my ways, skipping school, never doing homework, never preparing for exams. I drank and smoked and only cared about music and playing guitar. Really? I tried to avoid Ella and Dad. Ella was only around for three years before she died. I felt awful about it. I couldn't believe it. It made me think Dad was some sort of bad luck person. My mother died when I was only seven and then his second wife died after only three years of marriage."

"Do you recall anything about the time before the heist?" Ynes asked.

"Like what? How do you mean?"

"Did you notice anything different in the way my mother behaved? Was she worried about anything? Did she seem nervous?"

Erik let out a sigh. "I wouldn't have noticed if she did. I was consumed with myself. I didn't notice anything about anyone. I was completely self-centered back then. What do you think she worried about?"

"She had concerns about the museum's security. I wondered if her worries escalated right before the heist?"

"I really don't know."

"Have you ever heard Charles talk about who might have been involved in the heist? Has he ever talked about who might have killed my mother?"

"No. I've never heard anything like that." Erik looked out the window for a few seconds and then turned back to Ynes. "Do you remember that night?"

Ynes's eyebrows raised. "Not much."

Erik shook his head. "It was terrible. I was out late drinking with my buddies. We were jamming, enjoying the music, having a great time. I got home really late. It was a school night, but I didn't care. I was only in my room for about thirty minutes when I heard Dad in the living room. He sounded upset. I left my room to see what was wrong. He'd taken the call from the police telling him what had happened to Ella."

Ynes sat unmoving, her muscles tense and stiff.

"Dad was crying. He was so upset. He was angry, too, that this had happened, that he'd lost his wife. I don't recall what he said, but I barked at him. He slapped me across the face. Do you remember any of this?" Erik watched Ynes's face. "I remember you came down the hall from your bedroom and stood at the edge of the living room staring at us."

A flash of anxiety and fear washed over Ynes, but she kept her composure. "No, I don't remember that night." But something about Erik's words made her want to run from the room.

"I always wondered if you heard what Dad was saying to me." Erik's eyes bore into Ynes. "I felt badly if you heard about Ella from the hallway. It would have been an awful way to hear about your mother's death ... with Dad and I not getting along as usual. It made me feel terrible."

"I don't remember much of that night," Ynes said.

Olivia could see some tiny beads of perspiration on her friend's forehead.

"I don't even remember much about being told my mother was dead." Ynes ran her hand over her eyes.

"Did Dad tell you?" Erik asked.

"Tilly was with me. She held my hand and had her arm around me. I think Charles told me in the living room. You weren't there. I was very confused. I didn't really grasp what was going on. All I wanted was for my mother to come through the door and bring me back to bed." Ynes's voice cracked and a few tears slipped from her eyes.

Olivia asked Erik a question to give Ynes a minute to collect herself. "You graduated from high school shortly after the heist happened?"

Erik looked at Olivia like he'd forgotten she was there. "Yeah. That's right. About a month after."

"Your father told us you went to some outdoor program for the year following your graduation?"

"I did," Erik said. "I went kicking and screaming. They practically had to hogtie me. I had no intention of leaving Boston or my friends, but my father had different ideas. He made the arrangements without consulting me. I don't think I've ever been more enraged by anything. Dad went so far as to hire a bodyguard to look after me, to be sure I stayed with the program and didn't take off. I was there for ten months. Turns out, it was the best thing I could have done. It was the beginning of my turnaround."

Ynes cleared her throat. "You were pretty much gone from the house after you left for the outdoor program. Then you went to college. I barely saw you for those five years."

"I'm sorry we never really connected. There were so many years between us. After college, I went off to graduate school for two years and then started working here at the firm. You were at boarding school. We barely saw each other. I regret that." Erik looked Ynes. "Did Dad tell you I'm planning a run for office?"

Ynes blinked. "No, he didn't."

"I'm going to make a run for governor. I have a team. We're excited about it."

"Wow, governor? I didn't know."

Erik smiled. "Maybe you and I can start new, start over, build a strong relationship with each other. I'd like that. I really would."

Ynes nodded.

Olivia said, "You were away at school from the time you were eighteen until you completed your graduate work at around twenty-five. A lot went on in the investigation into the heist during that time. Did your father keep you up-to-date on the developments?"

Erik shrugged and shook his head. "Not really. He didn't bring it up much. He wanted me to focus on my work. He didn't want to distract me, I guess."

"Did you ask for information?"

Erik looked sheepish. "I didn't. I suppose I wanted to push it out of my life, not focus on sad things."

"Do you know much about what happened that night? Who might be involved?" Ynes asked.

Erik seemed to tense. "I don't. I should look into it, read about it. You've learned a lot? Dad said you've been immersing yourself in finding out information."

"I've read a good deal of the accounts, talked to some people."

Erik asked with interest, "Who have you talked to?"

"The museum director, the museum head of security, some people who knew my mom, a couple of criminals, the security guard who was on duty that night with my mother."

"Tim Mack? You talked to him?" Surprise sounded in Erik's voice.

"You remember the name?" Ynes asked.

"Sure. I heard Ella talk about him sometimes. I knew he got shot that night."

"Did you ever meet him?"

"Me? No."

Ynes said, "Mack was into the Boston music scene back then. I wondered if you'd ever met him."

"No. At least, I don't remember meeting him. I suppose I could have."

Ynes's face took on a grave expression. "I think someone who worked at the museum was involved in the heist."

Erik's eyes went wide. "Really? I never heard that. Someone in the museum was working with the criminals?"

"It's just what I think from what I've read."

"Does Dad think the same thing?" Erik asked.

"I'm not sure. He hasn't delved into the details like I have."

"I think Dad feels it's best left to law enforcement. I think he feels badly that he didn't ask Ella to leave the position."

Olivia asked, "Why would he want her to leave the museum job?"

"He didn't think she should be in a job like that. Working that late shift. Walking to her car in the dark."

"Did you hear them discuss those things?" Olivia questioned.

"Once in a while."

Ynes said, "I've heard over and over that my mother loved the Cooper, that she loved working there. I don't think Charles has to feel guilty that he never convinced her to give up the job. It was something my mother loved."

"Well, you know, in retrospect and all that. If Dad had asked Ella to stop working there, she'd still be alive." Erik looked down at his hands. "We all have things we regret not doing ... and things we regret doing."

17

Olivia and Ynes sat at the table in the condo with a laptop trying to find information about Tobey Sewall. Several old articles came up about the man reporting him as a low level Boston criminal who'd been arrested more than a few times for breaking and entering, petty theft, assault, selling drugs. The man had spent some time in prison. Information about him disappeared from the news a few months prior to the heist at the Cooper.

"Well, what happened to him?" Olivia asked as she hit more keys on the laptop. "He just up and disappeared?"

"Maybe he died," Ynes said.

"Wouldn't there be an obituary then?"

"Maybe he moved away," Ynes suggested.

Olivia leaned closer. "I'm searching on the name now without Boston or Massachusetts. If Sewall committed crimes or died or bought property or went to prison anywhere in the world, an article or a listing or a notice should come up. There's nothing."

"How can that be?" Ynes stared at the screen.

Olivia sighed. "Maybe he was abducted by aliens."

"Yes, likely," Ynes deadpanned. "So it's a dead end? Why did those guys drop that envelope in the parking lot then? Are they playing with us?"

Olivia tapped a pencil on the tabletop. "I doubt they were playing with us. Why go to the trouble?"

"How old was he in those articles from twenty years ago?" Ynes asked.

"Twenty-seven."

"Okay. So if he's still alive, he'd be about forty-seven."

"Maybe he's in prison," Olivia said. "Maybe he got a life sentence for something. He's been in prison all this time so he hasn't made any news."

"That makes the most sense of all." Ynes's face had questions written all over it. "But, why isn't there some article reporting on the crime that put him away for life?"

"Maybe we missed it." Olivia began to re-read the

many stories and listings that came up on the internet.

After another hour passed, the two friends gave up for the night. Ynes made tea and placed a mug in front of Olivia.

"What did you think about my stepbrother?"

Olivia sipped from her mug. "He said some nice things to you. He seems to want to build a relationship."

"I don't like him," Ynes said. "I didn't come right out and say it before the meeting because I didn't want to color your opinion."

Olivia smiled. "You didn't have to say it. I got the message over the years that you didn't like the guy."

"When Erik talked about the night my mother died, I got anxious. I felt sick. I could barely sit still. Some of the things he said sounded so familiar and other things I'd never heard, but even things that rang a bell for me seemed shrouded in a thick fog. I don't know if I remember any of it or if it's all things I was told when I was older."

"Do you recall standing near the living room and seeing Erik and your stepfather together?" Olivia asked.

"I don't know. Images swirl in my brain, but are they something I actually experienced or not?"

"Do you remember your stepfather slapping Erik?"

Ynes's heart began to race. "I don't know that either."

"Why don't you like Erik?"

Ynes took in a deep breath. "I have bad memories of him. He was always sneering at me. I was just a little kid so no wonder he didn't want anything to do with me. I remember tension in the household when he was around. I remember Charles yelling at him. I kept my distance from Erik. He made me nervous. We were two people living in the same house, but without any connection between us." Ynes looked at Olivia. "I didn't like him today either. He gives me a bad feeling. I don't feel like getting together with him. I don't want to build a relationship with him."

"Then don't," Olivia said.

"Really? I thought you'd encourage it."

"You were never really siblings," Olivia said. "You lived in the same house for three years, but he was much older and had nothing to do with you. Then he was gone to school and then you were gone to school. You and Erik don't have anything that ties you together. You don't have anything in common to hold onto. He gives you a negative feeling. There are millions of people in the world. Find the ones you like and build happy relationships with them. Move forward. Leave the past in the past."

Ynes wrapped her hands around her mug. "Are you telling me to drop my investigation into my mother's murder?"

"Last summer, I got involved in the cold case murders of my cousins from forty years ago," Olivia said.

"You solved it."

"It sort of solved itself. I just gave it a push."

"So you're *not* telling me to give up my investigating?"

"I think I learned some things from the summer. One being that justice is for the living, not the dead."

Ynes stared at Olivia.

"If you're doing all this for your mother, she doesn't care. It doesn't matter to her. If there is life after death, she's in a place where what happened to her here on earth doesn't really matter anymore. I imagine that place to be beautiful ... gentle, full of joy, free from care ... and forgiving."

Ynes bit her lip and said softly, "I don't know if I believe she doesn't care."

Olivia put her hand over her friend's and squeezed. "She cares about you. She wants you to be okay. Don't do all this for her sake."

When Ynes nodded, one tiny tear escaped from her eye and dropped onto the table. "I want the person who killed my mother to be named. I want the world to know who murdered my mother. That person stole her life from her. He stole from me, too. He got to live his life the past twenty years. I want that person to go to prison. I want the person to pay for what he did. That's the justice I want."

Olivia looked her friend in the eyes. "Then let's go get it."

18

Olivia entered the leather shop located across from Fenway Park. Her interaction with Randy, the man who created the beautiful boots and leather goods, had been picking at her for days. She'd left her phone number and email address with Randy's mother and the woman hadn't contacted her so there was no light to shed on his delivery to the townhouse where Ynes's acquaintance was killed. Even so. Olivia wanted to return to the store to see Randy again.

Paulina looked up from her work at the counter and smiled when she saw the young woman enter the store. "Olivia," she said as she walked out from behind the counter to meet her.

"I've been wondering how Randy was doing. When I was here earlier in the week, you told me he seemed 'off' that day. He showed some interest in interacting with me. Is he okay?"

Paulina's facial expression changed to one of concern. "Randy went out to pick up some sandwiches for our lunch. He'll be back any minute. He's been odd the past few days. I've been thinking about what you said about the murder of that woman in Beacon Hill. I asked Randy if he'd heard or seen anything that bothered him when he delivered that box. His face darkened and he left the room. He won't answer any questions about it."

"Does he seem upset?"

"Not exactly upset, I'd describe it as agitated. Not all the time, but a few times a day, he becomes sullen and grabs his sketchbook and draws feverishly for a while."

"Does he show you what he draws?"

"No." Paulina looked to the shop door. "But I took a look though his book when he wasn't around. I don't think we have time for me to show you. Randy will back soon." The woman took in a nervous breath. "Every page of the sketchbook contains drawings of that townhouse where the woman was killed. Two have a black line scrawled over them."

Olivia's breath caught in her throat. "Did you ask

him why he's drawing the townhouse?"

"No. He doesn't know I looked at the pictures. I can't address it unless he shows me or he'll know I looked at his book. Randy is very private and possessive of his artwork. He doesn't like anyone looking at his drawings until he's ready to show them."

"Will he eventually show them to you?"

"I don't know. I haven't seen him like this for ages." Paulina put her hand on the side of her neck and rubbed at the tension gathered there.

"Does Randy work with a therapist or a counselor?" Olivia asked.

"He sees a counselor once a month. His appointment is next week."

"What about a speech-language pathologist to help him with his communication? Does he see anyone for that?"

"He did for years. Now he meets with his speech therapist every two months or sooner if we have an issue we need help with. Maybe I should call her and ask her to come by."

Olivia said, "It might help. He has a relationship with those people. Maybe they can find out what he's feeling or what he's worried about. Sometimes, it's easier to open up to professionals than to a family member."

The door opened and the two women turned to see Randy coming into the shop carrying a brown paper bag with two sandwiches.

"Here he is now," Paulina said with forced cheerfulness. "Olivia came by to say hello."

Randy shut the door and stood still, his eyes glued to Olivia, a blank expression on his face.

"You brought back your lunch?" Olivia asked. "Don't let me keep you from eating. I was in the neighborhood and decided to come by, see how you're doing. Are you working on any new designs?"

Randy walked to the counter and opened the bag. He removed one of the sandwiches, opened the wrapping, took two paper plates from the bag and put half a sandwich on one and the other half on the second plate. Then he made eye contact with Olivia.

"Oh. Are you sharing your lunch with me?" Olivia smiled. "Thank you, Randy. You're very generous." Even though she didn't want to take part of the man's lunch, she didn't want to insult his kind gesture, so she accepted.

Randy picked up his half and headed for the back work room. He stopped at the threshold and looked back at Olivia, waiting for her. She scooped up her sandwich and followed the man to a table by the window.

Paulina brought her lunch and sat with them. "We usually sit here for lunch every day. We can watch the people walking around outside. Even when there isn't a game, there are often a lot of tourists who come by to see the baseball park, take pictures, walk around it."

"It's a great view." Olivia took a bite of the sandwich. "Delicious."

Randy ate his sandwich, occasionally looking up to take a glance at Olivia.

When the man had finished eating, he scrunched up the plate and napkin and got up to toss them in the trash can. He moved to his work table, picked up his notebook, and returned to the table where his mother and Olivia were sitting. He stood next to Olivia's chair.

Olivia noticed what he had in his hand. "Do you have some new designs? Do you want to show me?"

Randy sat down and placed the book in front of her. He opened it to a sketch of a boot. The leather was dark brown and on the side, there was an inset of roses engraved into a lighter-colored leather. The roses wound up the side of the boot.

Olivia admired the design. "It's gorgeous. I love it."

Randy turned the page to show a black leather

handbag with a flap cut on the diagonal with contrasting stitching around the edges. He went to the next page to show a leather jacket, fringe hanging down from below the shoulders and from the sleeves. Stars were cut out across the shoulders from the upper layer of leather.

Olivia loved each design and praised the original work. "You have an amazing talent."

Randy slid the sketchbook away from Olivia and folded his hands on top of it.

"Where did Randy learn his craft?" Olivia asked Paulina.

"He took classes at museums and from other artists. He took to the leather work right away. It seems he's a natural at it. I had the shop already, but we slowly moved the inventory to all leather goods when Randy showed an inclination for the work."

Paulina showed Olivia around the shop's work room with items in various stages of finish. "We have two other leather workers who we employ part time to work from Randy's designs. It's the only way we can keep up with the demand."

"Do you do the leather work, too?"

"I did for a little while. I prefer to handle the business end of things and leave the creative side to Randy."

Olivia looked to the lunch table where Randy was still sitting with his hands folded over the sketchbook. He was looking out the window at people passing by.

When the shop's bell rang indicating a customer had come in and Paulina went out to the front, Olivia went back to the table by the window. "Will you work on the products this afternoon or will you sketch some more designs?"

Randy seemed not to have heard the question. He just kept looking out of the window.

Olivia could see that his hands were clenching into fists and a wave of fear bubbled up inside of her. Had she made Randy angry somehow? Had he had enough of visiting with her? Was he thinking of something else?"

She took a step back and was about to go to the front of the store when Randy moved his head and shifted his gaze to his sketchbook.

"Are you tired, Randy? Shall I say goodbye and come visit another day?"

Randy didn't look up. He opened his book and flipped to the back of it. Paging through the sketches, he stopped at one of them and angled his body so that Olivia could look over his shoulder and see the drawing.

She had to stifle a gasp of surprise.

Randy had drawn Abigail Millett's brick Beacon Hill townhouse. The glossy black door was open in the picture. Part of the sparkling foyer chandelier was visible. Drops of bright red blood could be seen on the threshold.

"Is this what you saw when you made the delivery?" Olivia asked quietly.

Randy turned the page.

It was the townhouse again from a different view, from slightly further up the street. The door was open. The blood was on the entryway.

Randy turned the next page. The same drawing had been sketched on that page ... and on the next page, and the page after that. The focus in each picture was the black door, opened, and the drops of blood.

Olivia swallowed. "You saw the blood. You dropped the box you were delivering." She sat down next to Randy. "Did you hear anything? Did you see anything?"

Randy stared at the sketch and rubbed at his eyes with his fist. He leaned over and rested his head on the sketchbook.

Olivia said gently, "You're okay. You're safe. I'm going to go get your mother."

19

Sitting next to Ynes on the bus ride to Arlington to visit Tilly, the Cohen's housekeeper, Olivia couldn't stop thinking about Randy's drawings. Paulina planned to bring the sketchbook to Randy's next appointment with his counselor to see if any information might be gained. Paulina promised to let Olivia know the outcome.

Before the young women left Charles Cohen's townhouse in Boston after meeting with him the other day, Tilly had asked Ynes and Olivia to come to her house for coffee so she could catch up with Ynes. Since Tilly had the morning off, they made arrangements to meet at 9am.

Getting off the bus in the center of town, Ynes and Olivia walked for ten minutes to a side street of small, older, well-tended homes. Tilly and her husband lived in a white ranch with black shutters. Pots of colorful chrysanthemums lined the steps up to the front door and the window boxes spilled over with the same bright yellow flowers.

"Have you been here before?" Olivia asked.

"When I was a kid, Tilly had me over sometimes to bake cookies if my stepfather was going to be home late and the nanny he'd hired to take care for me had to go home. I haven't been here for years. It looks the same, clean, neat, like someone cares about the place and enjoys living here." Ynes rang the bell.

No one came to the door, so Ynes rang again.

Still no one answered.

Ynes pulled out her phone to check for a message from Tilly. "No message." She knocked hard against the door.

"Liv," Ynes's voice shook. "Something's wrong."

Olivia walked down the front steps to the front of the house and stood on tip-toes to see inside through the picture window. "There's too much glare. I can't see. Let's go around back."

Ynes knocked on the back door and leaned down to peer through the glass of the window into the kitchen. "Tilly!"

The older woman lay face-up on the floor.

Ynes grabbed the knob and turned. The door opened and she flew inside where she knelt next to Tilly. "She must have had a heart attack."

Olivia made an emergency call to request an ambulance, then knelt on the other side of the woman. She pressed her fingers to Tilly's neck. "There's a pulse. She's alive."

Ynes took the woman's hand in one of hers and gently ran the back of her other hand over Tilly's cheek.

Olivia spotted a coffee mug on the floor, its contents spilled over the tiles. Only one of Tilly's slippers was still on her foot.

Olivia stood and glanced around the room. The other slipper was on the far side of the kitchen as if Tilly had kicked it off.

Her heart beating double-time, Olivia scanned the room. "Would Tilly keep the back door unlocked?"

"What?" Ynes looked up at her friend.

"Was the back door unlocked when you tried it?" Olivia asked.

"Yes."

Olivia knelt beside the woman again and when she looked closely, her heart skipped a beat.

Small bruises had started to form on Tilly's neck.

The wail of an ambulance's siren could be heard approaching and in a few minutes, two EMTs entered through the back door. Ynes slid to the side out of the way. "She was on the floor when we arrived."

Olivia pointed and said to the medical personnel, "I think someone tried to strangle her. See the marks on the neck?"

With wide eyes, Ynes whirled to face her friend. "You think...?"

"Maybe." Olivia helped Ynes from the floor. "Ride with Tilly in the ambulance. I'm going to call for the police. I'll take a cab and meet you at the hospital."

TWO HOURS LATER, Olivia found Ynes sitting in the hospital waiting room. Tilly had regained consciousness, but had not spoken and faded in and out of sleep. Ynes had called the woman's husband and he and their two sons were in Tilly's room with her. The doctor told them she would be fine.

"That's a relief." Olivia sank into the chair next to Ynes.

"What did the police say?" Ynes asked.

"There was no sign of forced entry. They took some photos of the room and said they'd follow-up with the doctors. Did the physician speak about the marks on Tilly's neck?"

"Not to me." Ynes's eyes were bloodshot. "What happened back there?"

"I think either the back door was unlocked and someone went in, or Tilly knew the person and opened the door to him. Or the person picked the lock."

"You really think she was attacked?" Ynes pushed her hair back from her face.

Tilly's husband entered the waiting room and walked over to the young women. "Ynes, Tilly is awake. She's asking for you. I told Tilly you found her on the kitchen floor."

Ynes hurried to the room and stood by Tilly's bed holding her hand while Olivia waited near the door.

Tilly put one hand on her throat. Her voice was hoarse and tight when she spoke. The words came out in a croak. "Someone came into the kitchen from behind me. He grabbed me by the neck. He tried to strangle me."

Ynes asked softly, "Did you see his face?"

Tilly shook her head as her eyes filled with tears and she whispered, "He had something over his face." When she closed her eyes, Ynes moved back so the husband could comfort the woman.

As they were about to leave the room, the doctor took them aside. "We've called the police. They're on their way over. I understand you had them to the house?"

Olivia explained that she'd called the police and had explained her concerns to them. "They said they'd get in touch with me later."

After the discussion, the young women stepped out of the hospital lobby into the bright October sunshine and headed for the bus stop.

"Was the attack on Tilly random or was it because of me?" Ynes's voice was tight with emotion.

"The police will figure it out," Olivia said.

"Will they?" Ynes said with disgust. "They've spent twenty years trying to figure out who killed my mother."

They stood on the sidewalk waiting for the bus.

"What do you thing happened at Tilly's house?" Ynes asked.

Olivia sighed. "I think someone picked the lock and got in, or the door was unlocked. Tilly was in the kitchen. The guy grabbed her from behind and knocked her off balance. She struggled and one of her slippers flew off. The attacker strangled her and she lost consciousness. Either we interrupted the attack and the guy fled out the back door or he thought she was dead and he left her."

"Poor Tilly." Ynes moaned and put her hand on her throat. "It's because of me, isn't it?"

"Why though? What could Tilly know about the heist?" Olivia asked.

Ynes shrugged one of her shoulders.

"Did she ever bring up anything with you about the stolen art?"

"No."

"Anything about your mother being killed at the museum?"

"Gosh, no."

"Then the attack on Tilly could have been random," Olivia said.

Ynes gave her a skeptical look.

"Or not," Olivia added. "Why would someone attack Tilly? What does someone think she knows?"

"I have no idea. Tilly wasn't involved with the heist."

"Tilly worked for your stepfather for years?"

"She worked for him before my mother married Charles."

"Tilly and Charles must have a trusting relationship," Olivia guessed.

"Meaning?"

"Meaning, would Charles have confided in her?"

"No. Tilly was the *help*. That was always clear."

"Would Charles allow her to overhear a phone call or a conversation with a visitor or an associate?"

"Absolutely not. He would never conduct business with Tilly in the room."

Olivia asked, "Could she have found something incriminating in your father's office?"

Ynes blinked. "You think Charles knows something about the heist?"

Olivia hesitated. "When you asked your stepfather if he'd ever heard the name Tobey Sewall, I thought recognition flickered over his face for a millisecond. It was brief and then it was gone. I might be wrong and misinterpreted what I thought I saw, but I got the impression that he *had* heard the name."

"Oh no." Ynes wobbled and she looked like she might pass out.

Olivia maneuvered her friend to the bus stop bench. "I'm only speculating. I shouldn't have said anything."

"You could be right." Ynes's voice was almost inaudible. Her breath was coming fast and shallow. "Was Charles behind the heist? Money is everything to him. Was he the mastermind behind the robbery?"

"That is a huge leap. Let's not let our imaginations run away with us." Olivia sat down next to her friend and repeated the words Brad had spoken to her a few days ago. "We need to think things through logically."

Ynes looked at Olivia. "Who knew we were going to visit Tilly?"

"Tilly," Olivia said.

"My stepfather knew. He heard Tilly invite us." Ynes's eyes flicked around, focusing on nothing. "My stepbrother knew, too. I told him when we met with him."

Olivia suggested, "Tilly might have told someone. She seemed to be really looking forward to talking with you. She must have told people you were going to visit."

"My head is spinning." Ynes swallowed hard. "What could Tilly know that someone wouldn't want her to talk to me about? It doesn't make any sense."

"Tilly was working for your stepfather and your mother. She was in their employ before the heist and afterwards," Olivia pointed out. "Maybe she heard something your mother said about someone.

Maybe your mother confided something to Tilly. It might be something that Tilly doesn't even realize is important. But someone else thinks it is."

Ynes said, "I'm pretty sure Abigail Millett got killed because she was researching the heist. Someone broke into Abigail's Beacon Hill townhouse and stabbed her to death because of something she was on to. Someone went to Tilly's and tried to kill her because they knew I was coming to see her. What did Abigail and Tilly know?"

Olivia narrowed her eyes as anxiety rushed through her body. "Another important question is ... does this person think *you* know the same information that Abigail and Tilly know?"

Ynes met her friend's gaze with a wide-eyed look of fear.

20

Ynes had twice emailed Abigail Millett's daughter, Denise Millett Spencer, offering condolences and asking if they might meet. She received a reply inviting her to come to Denise's law office in Hingham. The office was located on North Street near several restaurants, a café, and the public library.

"I'm sorry I didn't reply to your message sooner," Denise said as she led the way down the hall to her office. "There was so much to organize. We had a private service with only a few close friends and the family. It's all been a whirlwind."

Denise, an attorney, was about five foot six, slim and athletic-looking, in her late-thirties, with shoulder-length sandy-blond hair. She wore a tan skirt and matching blazer.

Ynes, Olivia, and Denise took comfortable chairs in front of a fireplace in the cozy, but professionally-decorated office space. "It's really unbelievable what happened to my mother." Denise let out a sigh. "I understand you're doing some research on the Cooper art heist. My mother mentioned your name once or twice. She told me your mother died protecting the art. I know it was nearly twenty years ago, but I'm very sorry about it."

"Thank you," Ynes told the woman. "That's very kind of you."

Denise asked, "You mentioned that you and my mother would occasionally share information about the heist. Do you think the attack on my mother was because of her research?"

"I'm worried that's the reason," Ynes said. "Did your mother tell you what she was working on? Did she tell you about something she'd recently learned?"

Denise shook her head. "She didn't talk much about her work. Once in a while, it might come up, but we mostly talked about family things, what we were doing with friends, upcoming plans."

Olivia's heart dropped in disappointment. She's hoped to learn what Abigail Millett had uncovered that had pushed someone to take her life. "Did your mother mention anyone she'd recently interviewed or spoken with in regards to the heist?"

Denise took a deep breath and took a few moments to think back on her conversations with her mother. "Nothing comes to mind. I always worried about her speaking to certain people to gather information for this project. I feared she might step on someone's toes or make someone angry or get too close to a discovery that someone wouldn't be pleased about. I told her it was a dangerous thing to be researching. She didn't think so. She'd tell me the heist was twenty years ago ... the statute of limitations for theft was up ... some people involved were old or had died. She really didn't have any concerns." Denise lifted her hands in a helpless gesture. "I had concerns and I voiced them, but it didn't stop her."

Olivia asked, "Your mother didn't talk about any worries she had recently? She wasn't worried about her safety? There were no indications that she'd been threatened or warned away from something?"

"If there were warnings, she didn't share them with me or other members of the family. Believe me, I asked." Denise's face was serious.

"After what happened, did you look at the working manuscript of her book?" Ynes asked.

"I did. She was working on a chapter about things that had been overlooked by law enforcement like not bringing in the assistance of beat cops who were familiar with the criminals and gangs back then ... things like that. Those things weren't anything new. She had those notes from the beginning of her research. She seemed to be organizing that information into a separate chapter."

"What about her phone records?" Olivia asked. "Anything unusual about them? Calls to or from someone she hadn't spoken with previously?"

"The phone records didn't show anything of concern," Denise said.

"Phone records can sometimes show a person's location," Olivia said. "What about locations she would be unlikely to visit? Like abandoned buildings, questionable neighborhoods, places you wouldn't expect her to be?"

"The police are looking at that information ... places she'd been ... times she was there. So far, I haven't been asked or told about any places that seemed questionable ... or why my mother would be in certain locations." Denise looked at Ynes. "Have you found any recent information you think could be linked to my mother's death?"

Ynes blinked. "Unfortunately, no. I wish I had something to offer that would lead to her killer."

Olivia made eye contact with Ynes and gave a slight nod.

Ynes said, "I haven't been in Boston for about two years. The year after my mother died, my stepfather moved us to London. I lived there until I returned to Boston for college. I went back to England for my master's studies and I've been working in Washington, D.C. for the past few months in an internship position. I came back here for two weeks to look into the heist to try to find information about my mother's killer."

Ynes cleared her throat and continued. "I visited my stepfather who now lives in Boston once again. His housekeeper, Tilly, invited me to her home for coffee and to talk. She's been with my father for decades and she helped to raise me along with my nannies. When Olivia and I arrived at her house, we found her on the floor, unconscious."

Denise let out a gasp of surprise.

Ynes went on, "She was attacked in her kitchen. Someone tried to kill her by strangulation. Tilly is in the hospital and is expected to make a full recovery."

Olivia said, "We suspect someone was trying to keep Tilly from talking to Ynes."

"Why would someone do that now? It's been so long since the heist took place," Denise said.

"We think it's because Ynes has been looking into the crime," Olivia said. "She's been asking questions, meeting with people, trying to figure out who killed her mother. As you probably know, there is no statute of limitations on murder. Maybe Ynes is getting too close. Maybe Tilly's attacker thought the housekeeper had something to reveal to Ynes."

"Wow," Denise muttered and then turned to face Ynes. "It seems the renewed interest in the crime from my mother and from you might have someone very worried." The woman's eyes widened. "You know, my mother mentioned that she'd spoken with the guard who was on duty at the Cooper on the night of the murder. You mentioning that you'd been working in D.C. must have triggered my memory. My mother told me the guard had been living in the D.C. area and was going to move back to Boston. She'd met with him in D.C. just before she died."

"Tim Mack?" Ynes asked.

"That's the man." Denise nodded.

Alarm bells went off in Olivia's head. Did Tim Mack reveal something new to Abigail Millett? Did he point a finger at someone? If he did, how would the person know what Mack had told Ms. Millett?

Olivia suddenly sat up straight. "Did your mother keep notebooks? Did she use notebooks to take down information?"

"She did." Ynes looked excited. "The few times we met, your mother had a notebook with her. She'd flip through the pages to report information to me."

Denise said, "My mother liked to take notes and then transfer the most salient points to the document on her laptop. I put her notebooks into boxes. They're still in her townhouse."

"Was she working in a notebook at the time of the attack?" Olivia's face wore an expression of concern.

"I'm sure she was. That's how she did things," Denise said.

Olivia looked from Denise to Ynes. "The attacker may have stolen her notebook."

"I don't think so. Not unless she was working at the time of the attack," Denise said. "When she wasn't working, my mother kept her laptop and her notebooks in a safe. She was paranoid about losing her work. When she was a college student, one evening when she was out with friends, her apartment building went up in flames and my mother lost all of her work in the fire. It stuck with her. She always used the safe for her research. My mother's laptop was in the safe so I think we can assume her most current notebook was in there, too. I'll go to the townhouse over the next few days and take a look. I'll let you know."

Ynes thanked Denise.

Olivia asked, "Did your mother think the paintings would be found and returned to the Cooper?"

"It was her hope and her wish," Denise said. "She did have concerns that the paintings had not been properly stored since the theft. To find the artwork and discover they'd been ruined would have broken her heart."

"I've heard lots of rumors about where the paintings might be," Ynes said. "Did your mother have any recent hunches about where the art might be stored?"

"She went back and forth about that, but last year, somebody brought it up at a holiday get-together and I distinctly recall her saying she was certain the paintings were still in the country. In fact, she was pretty sure the majority of the paintings were still in Massachusetts."

"Really? Did she say where? In a storage facility? In a private collection?" Olivia asked.

"There were a lot of people at the gathering. The conversation quickly turned to something else. I think people thought she might be joking. Somebody made a joking remark and everyone laughed and that was the end of it. I always meant to ask her more about what she thought." Denise frowned and shrugged. "I missed my chance, unfortunately."

Olivia said, "Maybe your mother's answer will be in the notes she took ... and so carefully stored in her safe."

21

Ynes and Olivia sat opposite Tilly who rested in a chair next to her hospital bed with a blanket over her legs. Tilly's husband had brought cups of tea and a box of cookies in for them and then disappeared so they could chat.

Bruises and deep brownish ligature marks showed on the woman's neck. Her fingertip moved slowly over the line where someone had wrapped a cord and tightened it with the intention of strangling Tilly to death.

"I still can't believe it." Tilly looked a little pale and tired, but her eyes were alert and focused. "Whatever made him stop choking me, saved my life. He must have heard you two at the front door. If the timing was different...." The housekeeper shook her head and let her voice trail off.

"But the timing *wasn't* different," Ynes said soothingly. "We came to the door and the monster ran off. And you're here with us."

"Thank the good Lord for that," Tilly said, her finger still touching her neck.

"You didn't see the man's face?" Ynes asked.

"No. I wish I did." Tilly's lips pulled down at the corners. "I was in the kitchen. I'd put the cake on a pretty platter and was about to go to the cupboard for the nice mugs. I heard something behind me and was about to turn, but the man whipped that cord over my head and started to pull. I lost my balance and fell back against him." Tilly put her hand over her heart. "I was sure I'd have a heart attack. Silly ... that thought running through my head. I would have been strangled to death before I had a heart attack."

"Did you fight him?" Ynes asked. "Did you even have time to fight against him?"

"I grabbed at the cord around my neck. I tried to reach back to poke him in the eye. I thrashed around trying to kick him with my heel, but I couldn't manage to hit him. My vision started to go. People say they see stars ... it was sort of like that ... twinkling at the edges of my vision. I was fighting, but it wasn't any use. Everything went black. I woke up in the hospital."

Ynes got up and went to sit on the bed closer to Tilly. She took the woman's hand and held it tightly. "You are one strong lady."

Tilly said with conviction, "I wish I'd have been stronger so I could've gotten a look at that monster's face."

"Was the back door unlocked?" Olivia asked.

"No way." Tilly shook her head hard. "If I'm alone in the house, the doors are always locked."

"So he must have picked the lock," Olivia said.

"He must have been good at it and he must have been quick because I didn't hear him or see him at the door. I'd been in and out the kitchen for at least fifteen minutes."

"He didn't steal anything?" Olivia asked.

"That was probably his intention," Tilly said, "but you got here and chased him away before he could take anything."

"I wonder," Ynes said and Tilly turned to look at the young woman.

"What do you wonder, hon?" Tilly had a questioning look on her face.

"I've been looking into the Cooper Museum art heist," Ynes said.

Tilly shrunk a little. "Why?"

Ynes explained how in her senior year of college she began to really think about what had happened to her mother. "It hit me in a strange way. I felt like I'd lost her all over again. I thought about her life, how I was the same age she was when she had me. I felt depressed and despondent and then I decided to find out everything I could about the heist and who was involved. I searched for information and ate it up."

Tilly patted Ynes's hand. "Your mother was a fine lady."

A half-smile formed over Ynes's mouth. "You liked her? Did you talk to her much?"

"Oh, my, yes. Your mother never made me feel like I was just the housekeeper. She talked to me like a friend. Appreciated me as a person. Sometimes, in the afternoons, we'd sit in the kitchen and have a cup of tea. We'd talk and laugh. If your stepfather ever saw us, he would have had a word with Ella. With him, lines didn't cross. I was the help. I wasn't supposed to socialize or be too friendly with the family. Ella didn't treat me like that." Tilly shook her head slowly, thinking back twenty years. "Your mother was kind and caring and funny and intelligent. How I loved her. I considered her a dear friend." Tilly made a little noise in her throat. "I almost quit right after your mother died. It was hard to be in that house without her around."

"Why did you change your mind?" Ynes asked. "Why did you stay?"

"For you." Tilly smiled. "You had a terrible loss in your life. I wasn't going to leave you and add to your loss."

The woman's words squeezed at Ynes's heart. "You moved to England with us," Ynes said it like she'd just realized how hard that must have been.

"Yup, we did. Our kids were out of the house. Miles thought it would be a great adventure. Your father hired Miles to be caretaker of the property, so off we went across the pond. We never regretted it."

"I was six when we left for London. I didn't understand what a big deal that would have been for you and Miles. You were always around. I thought you'd always be around. I never thought you wouldn't be with me."

Tilly hugged Ynes. "Nannies came and went. A child needs stability."

"Erik wasn't happy about Charles moving to

London," Ynes said. "I remember his fussing and how angry he was about it."

"Your brother was not an easy young man," Tilly said. "I'm glad he turned himself around."

"I got together with Erik the other day," Ynes said.

"Did you?"

"He's never felt like a brother to me. We never connected. Part of it was the age difference between us. Part of it was ... I don't know."

"Like I said," Tilly told Ynes, "Erik was never an easy person to be around back then."

"I've never felt like Charles was my father either," Ynes confessed. "He's always been nice and kind, but I've never felt like he loved me. He never seemed to know what to do with me. I always felt I was in the way."

"I believe Charles loves you, hon. He's a businessman. Children were hard for him. He was sort of awkward. He never could say the right thing, he never knew how to act, how to show his love to children."

Ynes said, "You were at the townhouse the night my mother died. Why hadn't you gone home?"

"You'd had a fever all day. Your nanny called out that day, too. Charles had a late meeting and Ella had to work that night. She asked if I'd stay over and watch you. I did that from time to time. I'd stay in the guest room."

"I remember that. How did you find out my mother had been killed?"

Tilly sighed. "Erik and Charles were in the living room. Their loud talking woke me. Actually, it was their *yelling* that woke me. I opened my bedroom door to listen. I thought I heard something about your mother so I grabbed my robe and headed to the living room to see what was going on. As I was about to walk in, your stepfather slapped Erik across the face. They yelled some more and then Charles saw me. I asked him if something had happened to Ella. He was distraught. He said she'd been killed. I almost fainted and then I noticed you. You were behind a chair. I scooped you up. You still had the fever. I wasn't sure if you'd heard what Charles had said or not. I brought you back to your room. Did you hear what Charles said?"

"I don't think I heard him say my mother had been killed, but I'm not sure. I remember feeling like I was in a fog. That must have been from the fever." A thought slipped into Ynes's brain. "I remember being confused about something he said." She looked at Tilly. "But, I think I remember Charles saying something to Erik like ... you are my only child ... you are my only child ... why are you behaving like this? Something like that. Did Charles say that?"

Tilly's face was ashen. "Charles didn't mean anything by that. He didn't mean he only had one child. He was upset. He wasn't making a lot of sense." The woman shook her head. "I was afraid you'd heard him say that. I was afraid you were hurt by what he said. You had a funny look on your face, a look of confusion."

Olivia noticed Ynes stiffen and her eyes darken. "I think I heard Charles say my mother was dead. I thought it was day-time when he told me though. Weren't we sitting together in the living room?"

"It was just after dawn. You got up again. Charles was in the living room. I sat with you and held your hand. Charles told you your mother had been killed in an accident."

Ynes looked down at her hands. "Yes," she whispered. "When I saw Erik the other day, he told me he'd been out that night with his friends until very late. He'd gotten home about thirty minutes before Charles got the news. He told me they had an argument. You must have heard them arguing. That was what woke you up."

"It must have been," Tilly said.

"You didn't hear Erik sneak in?" Ynes asked.

"I don't think so. I slept lightly that night listening for you in case you were getting worse, but I don't recall hearing Erik in the hall."

"Do you know why Erik and Charles were fighting that night?" Ynes asked.

"I don't."

Olivia looked at her friend. "Do *you* know why they were fighting that night?"

"If I did, I don't remember why any longer." Ynes blinked several times, thinking, and then she looked at Tilly. "That man who broke in here and tried to hurt you. What if it wasn't a random attack?"

Tilly tilted her head in question not understanding what Ynes meant. "You mean the man intentionally attacked *me*? Why would he? What could be the reason?"

"He might think you know something about the Cooper Museum heist," Olivia told the woman.

"Me?" Tilly's cheeks reddened. "What would I know?"

Olivia said, "You worked for Charles and Ella. Ella worked at the museum. Did you ever hear Ella complaining about security or about someone who worked there?"

"Sure. She thought the security was lax and it needed to be beefed up. She thought one of the guards didn't give the job the seriousness it deserved. I don't know any specifics about her concerns. Why would someone think I did? I'm just the housekeeper."

Olivia was pretty certain that someone thought Tilly knew something ... something important.

22

———

"Do you think Tilly knows something and isn't being forthcoming about it?" Olivia sipped some wine from her glass. A vegetable stew simmered on the stove and cornbread baked in the oven.

"She might know something, but I don't believe she thinks it has anything to do with finding the robbers or my mother's killer." Ynes stirred the stew with a wooden spoon. "I don't think she would deliberately hide what she knows. I think she'd go right to my stepfather and to the police with the information."

"I would bet that the person who tried to kill Tilly thinks she has important information," Olivia said. "And is afraid she's going to share that information with you."

"What could Tilly know? If my mother knew anything about the heist, she wouldn't have gone to work that night," Ynes said. "She would have alerted the police."

Olivia stared at the dark red wine and moved her glass so the liquid moved gently from side to side. "I don't know. Something is right under our noses."

"Well, let me know if you manage to sniff it out." Ynes took the cornbread out of the oven and set it to the side to cool. She sat at the small table across from Olivia. "Time's running out. I have to go back to Oxford soon."

"That doesn't mean you have to give up on your sleuthing. So much is online and more and more becomes available all the time. You can keep investigating from England," Olivia encouraged.

Ynes rested her chin in her hand. "I remember my stepfather saying he only had one child, and that child was Erik. He didn't consider me part of the family. I was an outsider. His words the night my mother was killed served to highlight what I'd always felt."

"It was twenty years ago. You had a fever that night. You might not have heard him correctly."

"Tilly heard the same thing I heard."

"When Charles was speaking to Erik he might have said he had only one *son*, not only one child."

"Liv. I heard him."

"Charles was upset. He was angry. His wife had just been killed. His life had been turned upside down. He probably misspoke. I don't think you can consider what he said as fact. I don't believe he meant how it came out."

Ynes sat up and moved her hand in the air in a dismissive way. "It came out of his mouth and that has been my impression of our relationship. It is what it is. I can't wave a magic wand and make things the way I wish they could be."

Olivia didn't know what to say so they sat in silence for a few minutes.

"What could Erik have said to Charles that night that made Charles slap him?" Ynes asked.

"Erik had probably been drinking. He came home in the wee hours of the morning. When he heard about your mother, he might have said something stupid or dismissive and Charles went ballistic."

"Maybe," Ynes said. "When we met with Erik the other day, when he brought up that night, my body flooded with anxiety. Talking about it with Erik made me feel ill."

"All the sensations you experienced that night rushed back," Olivia said. "You were a little kid, plus you had a fever. At that age, you didn't have the capacity to deal with what you heard. Your memory is awash in the emotion of it all."

Ynes ladled the stew into bowls and cut the cornbread.

"Charles is a multimillionaire, probably close to a billionaire," Ynes said. "Why doesn't he use some of that money to get to the bottom of the heist? Try to find out who was behind it. Try to find the art. Try to find out who killed my mother."

"Maybe he has and nothing has worked out."

"I don't know." Ynes blew out a breath. "He's never even hinted that he's bankrolling an investigation. Can you imagine what might be possible with a big fat bank account like Charles has? Money talks ... it gets results," Ynes had made an appointment to see a former Boston police officer and intended to have him spread the word that she had money to spend if anyone wanted to share information with her. She'd told Olivia that her trust fund might be useful in bringing some people forward.

After finishing the meal, Ynes said, "Want to go out for a while? I'm feeling cooped up and antsy. There's a nice Irish pub a couple of blocks from here. They have live music most nights. It would be nice to stop thinking about everything for a couple of hours."

Olivia smiled and got up to get her jacket. "You don't have to ask me twice."

OLIVIA AND YNES found a high table near the bar that some people had just vacated. They each sipped a beer and tapped their feet to the energetic music of the four-man band. Two people got up and danced a jig next to their table and most of the customers clapped in time to the beat and cheered the couple on.

"This is just what I needed." Ynes looked happy and bright and like a huge weight had been lifted from her shoulders ... for a short time anyway.

Olivia nodded and smiled in agreement.

When the band took a break, people jostled around to get to the bar and a well-dressed man in a suit bumped into Olivia's back.

"Sorry," the man told her and then he noticed Ynes. "Ynes?"

Ynes turned, but didn't recognize the man.

"Paul. I'm Paul Betts. I was a friend of your

brother. I met you a few years ago when you were in college. My sister, Jessie, was in your class year."

Ynes's face brightened. "Of course. I remember." She reached across the table to shake hands and then introduced Olivia. "How's Jessie?"

"She's in med school now." Paul asked what Ynes was doing and she told him she was at Oxford doing master's work.

"Great band, isn't it?" Paul said. "I haven't seen your brother in years. Erik was a terrific musician. What's he up to now?"

"Erik is a senior vice president at my stepfather's company," Ynes reported.

"I guess the apple doesn't fall far from the tree," Paul smiled. "I was sure he'd do something with music. He was so talented."

"Did you play?" Olivia asked.

"I played guitar and keyboards. Erik and I were in high school together. I was nowhere as good as Erik, that guy could play." Paul shook his head in admiration. "I learned a lot from him and the other guys we jammed with. There were groups all over the city who would get together to play informally. It was a good time." Paul let out a laugh. "We'd play in all kinds of places ... people's apartments, garages, basements.

We'd meet in a middle school sometimes where one of the guys worked. He had a key and would let us all in late at night. We played in the classrooms, in the auditorium. We even went to the Cooper Museum and played in there some nights. We'd bring beer, smokes, our instruments. Had a great time."

Ynes almost choked on her swallow of beer. She stared at Paul with wide eyes. "You played in the Cooper? Was my brother with you?"

"Yeah, he was. I know, right? We were crazy back then."

"How'd you get into the museum after hours?" Olivia asked, but thought she probably knew the answer.

"One of the guards. He was a musician. He was in a band. I thought he might make it big one day. He was a really good guitarist."

"When did you do this?" Ynes kept her voice even.

"I was a senior in high school," Paul said. "Some of the other guys were in their mid to late-twenties. We were risk takers back then. We could have gotten arrested. I'd never do that stuff now."

"Who was the guard who let you into the Cooper?" Olivia asked.

"A guy named Tim Mack. He was in a band called Winding Road."

Olivia and Ynes exchanged a look.

"I wonder if they ever made any records. I wonder what ever happened to them," Paul said.

"Nothing probably," Ynes said. "I've never heard of them. How often did you and Erik play in the Cooper?"

"Oh, let's see. A dozen times? It was in the winter and early spring of senior year. I didn't go after that. My parents found out and that was the end of that. Maybe Erik kept going? I don't know. Anyway, it was a great time."

"How many of you used to jam together?" Olivia asked.

"Sometimes five or six. Sometimes ten or eleven. It depended on the night."

"You knew all the guys?" Ynes asked.

"A few of us were from high school, but most were older guys in their twenties. I got to know them from playing together. Not best friends or anything, it was purely for practice and to be around other musicians." Paul waved across the room at some people. "I see my buddies. Nice talking to you. Tell Erik hello for me." He maneuvered his way through the crowd.

"Erik played in the Cooper late at night." Ynes's face was like stone. "His senior year of high school. Shortly before the heist took place."

"Those musicians didn't have anything to do with the heist." Olivia tried to calm Ynes down. "They're lucky they weren't playing in there on the night of the robbery."

"Maybe they *were* in there that night." Ynes's eyes narrowed. "What if one of the musician guys let those fake cops in thinking they were legit police officers. Maybe Tim Mack has been covering for them for the past twenty years ... protecting them." Ynes's lips were squeezed together in a thin line.

A million questions washed over Olivia like a tsunami. "We need to talk to Tim Mack again."

23

Olivia and Ynes met Mike Reilly, a retired Boston police officer, in a café in the Back Bay. The man was grey-haired, medium height, with a slight paunch. He had a kind, friendly face and he stood to shake hands when the young women arrived.

"Nice to meet, ya. I got here early."

Ynes's friend who worked for the FBI out of the D.C. office put her in contact with Mike Reilly reporting the man was a wealth of knowledge about the Cooper heist.

Reilly said, "My brother, Max, was a reporter for a city paper when the heist took place. He wrote quite a few stories over the years about the robbery and the loss of the paintings. He contributed to a book on the subject. Max passed away two years ago, otherwise he'd be here to talk with you, too."

"We appreciate you meeting with us," Olivia told the man.

"I understand you're both pretty well-versed in the history of the case. I hope I can tell you something you don't already know." Reilly raised his mug and took a swallow of his coffee.

"We learned recently that a bunch of musicians would sometimes gather at the Cooper for late night jam sessions," Olivia said.

Reilly rolled his eyes. "It's true. It went on for months. Not every night, of course, maybe once a week. The museum director got wind of it and docked the pay of the security guard who allowed the group in. We'd go by every once in a while and if they were in there playing, we'd kick them out. The last time it happened, we told them we'd arrest them for trespassing if we ever caught them in there again. We were serious, too. The director had had enough. The guard would unlock the back entry door so they could come in. There were rumors that the Cooper might be hit by thieves. We didn't need those musicians in there if a robbery took place."

"When did you threaten the group with arrest?" Olivia asked.

Reilly blew out sigh. "The night before the heist. We kicked them out around 11pm or so."

"Was Tim Mack the guard who let the musicians in?" Ynes asked.

"Yeah, it was Tim. He was a guitarist. A pretty good one, too. He had worked at the museum for years, but got to the point where he didn't care anymore. He felt like the museum directors and the board didn't take the security issues seriously so he decided to stop caring himself. I spoke to the guy several times. He had a point. It was wrong to be so lax in his job, but I understand his frustration with the management of the security process."

"We've read about the rumors that the museum would be hit," Olivia said. "Were those rumors taken seriously?"

"The police force took them seriously." Reilly nodded. "We had it on good information that a hit was coming. I think the museum directors pooh-poohed the news. Maybe they thought the security was fine and could handle a situation. I never conversed directly with any of them. My brother always said it was money that had held back any upgrades."

"Do you know who was involved in the heist?" Ynes asked, leaning slightly forward in her seat.

"Do you mean the mastermind or the grunts who did the work of it?" Reilly asked.

"Both? Either?" Ynes answered.

"The thought is that a Boston mob boss directed the heist, Billy Martin. His group worked occasionally with a group of thugs under the thumb of a guy named Jimmy Faber."

"We've met Faber," Olivia said with distaste.

Reilly's eyebrows went up. "Yeah, a piece of work that guy. Useless. In his eighties now. It might be time to make amends for the things he's done, but no dice. The guy won't talk ... says he doesn't know a thing. Sure, he doesn't." Reilly shook his head in disgust. "Supposedly, Billy Martin had the artwork stored here in Massachusetts. He didn't want it moved out of state. The theory is Billy had the art stolen to use in a deal to get a buddy of his off death row. For whatever reasons, the deal was never completed. Before he died, Billy gave Jimmy Farber three pieces of the stolen art. Other people have told law enforcement the same thing, that Jimmy has some of the art. Jimmy says no."

"When the deal for his friend didn't work out, why didn't Billy Martin sell the paintings?" Olivia asked.

"A combination of things. It isn't easy to find a

broker for a deal like that. Sure, there are private people who would be interested in purchasing some of the artwork, but the news of that heist was all over the world. People wanted to lay low. The other theory is that Billy Martin loved the Cooper. When he was a kid, in the winter, he'd skip school and go to the Cooper to stay warm. Ole' Billy loved that museum. He loved the art. Billy decided he didn't want to sell the paintings."

"Really?" Ynes asked. "Millions of dollars-worth of art and he wasn't tempted to sell?"

"Billy had plenty of money," Reilly said. "Millions. He was getting older. Supposedly, he told people he didn't care about money any more. He could never spend all he had. Other things were more important to him ... power, respect, his pals, his family, his legacy."

"How noble," Ynes spat. "All his lofty ideals. Where were his ethics when he was acquiring all that money? Other people's *lives* didn't matter to him then."

"These people aren't like others," Reilly said quietly. "They go after what they want, others be damned."

"Billy Martin is dead," Olivia said. "Who controls the paintings now?"

"Martin had two sons and a daughter. The sons didn't want anything to do with the family business. The daughter, Eliza, didn't either. They inherited old Billy's wealth and assets though. The thought is that the daughter is now in charge of the artwork and she believes it's time for the paintings to be returned. There are members of Billy Martin's 'group' who don't agree. Therefore, a battle is going on."

Ynes asked, "If the police or the FBI know all this, why didn't they go after Billy years ago? Why don't they go after the daughter now?"

"Eliza Martin didn't have anything to do with the crime. Through the grapevine, law enforcement knows Eliza is trying to return the paintings to the Cooper. Eliza has to butt heads with some people first. If the police go in now, the sensitive dealings will get squashed and the paintings might be destroyed or broken up and sold overseas. Remember, no one in law enforcement knows where the stolen artwork is located."

"But what about years ago," Ynes pressed. "Why didn't they go after Billy Martin back then?"

"For some of the same reasons ... everyone wants the artwork returned. The loss of those paintings is a loss for humanity, not just for the Cooper, not just for the people of Boston ... it is a loss for the world.

No one wants to make a mistake, push someone too far, ruin any chances of the paintings being returned. There were times when it seemed so close ... and then something would happen to crush those hopes. Over and over again, it happened." Sadness tugged at Reilly's face.

Ynes swallowed. "What about the men who took part in the heist? Do you know their names?"

"That's a more difficult question to answer," Reilly said. "Names have been bandied about over the years, but nothing has stuck."

Ynes seemed to deflate. "You know about the woman murdered in her Beacon Hill townhouse, Abigail Millett?"

Reilly nodded.

Ynes said, "I think her death is linked to the Cooper case. Abigail was working on a book about the heist. I think she found out some information that someone didn't want her to know."

"I've heard that," Reilly said.

"The housekeeper who worked for my stepfather for more than twenty years had an attempt on her life recently. Someone tried to strangle her."

Reilly sat up straight. "I didn't hear that. You're thinking there's a connection to the Cooper case?"

Ynes said, "I think someone was afraid that the

housekeeper knew something and was about to tell me what she knew. I've been researching the heist. I think Abigail Millett and I have been shining too bright a light on someone."

Reilly scratched the back of his neck. "You might want to be careful."

"Any ideas about who might be so desperate to keep his secrets that he'd kill one person and attempt to silence another?" Ynes asked.

"Those questions have been asked for decades. Lots of people have researched the case over the years. What's different this time?" Reilly thought out loud.

"That's what we're hoping to find out," Olivia said.

"I think the fussing going on right now between gangs over the return of the paintings is playing a part in making some people desperate about information leaking, names being mentioned." Reilly looked from Olivia to Ynes. "There's a guy you might want to talk to. He was involved in the city's crime world back around the time the Cooper was hit. He's turned his life around since then. Gave up the gangs and the crime and the mess of that world. I don't bring him up to people. He doesn't want to talk about the way things used to be. I'm going to make an exception. I'll give you his email address. I'll give him a call so he knows who you are. His name is Tobey. Tobey Sewall."

Ynes's and Olivia's mouths dropped.

Olivia explained how a man told them to go to an isolated lot in Quincy where a car drove up and dropped an envelope on the ground. "Inside the envelope was a piece of paper with that name on it. We tried to look him up, but all information about him stopped twenty years ago."

"His real name is Anthony Sewall ... Anthony Tobias Sewall." Reilly made eye contact with Ynes. "Tell Tobey who your mother was. He might be able to help you a little. I'm emphasizing the words *might* and *a little*. Don't expect a lot, but it's worth a chance. Go and see him."

24

Anthony Tobias Sewall was tall and lanky which made him, at first glance, appear younger than he was. The man had graying hair and dark brown piercing eyes. He looked to be in his early fifties, but his age was hard to pinpoint from his appearance.

The day was warm and sunny, one of those Indian summer days that feel so good following the cooler autumn weather. Sewall wore jeans and a t-shirt and when he saw the two young women approaching, he set down the unopened paint can he was holding and started down the driveway to meet them.

"Tobey Sewall." He shook with them.

"It's a beautiful house." Olivia admired the old Victorian even though it was in need of some care.

"I bought it recently. Planning to spruce it up and bring it back to life." Sewall looked at the front porch. "Care to have a seat on the porch?"

Four white rockers sat on the covered porch of the house and Olivia, Ynes, and Sewall made themselves comfortable.

"I hear you have some questions for me." The man rocked easy, back and forth.

Ynes told the man how she'd been researching the Cooper Museum case. "My mother was the security guard who was killed during the heist."

Sewall's eyes narrowed when he heard Ynes's comment. "How old were you when your mother died?"

"I was five."

"Do you remember her?"

"Little things. Her smile, the way she smelled of flowers and citrus. I remember holding her hand. I remember snippets and images of a day at the beach, at the grocery store together. Hugs, and her reading to me." Ynes took in a long breath.

"She was married to Charles Cohen?"

"Yes."

"He isn't your biological father?"

"No."

Sewall gave a little nod. "Why are you investigating now?"

"I want to know who killed my mother."

"For purposes of revenge? What are you planning to do with the information? Kill the guy?"

"I'd *like* to kill the guy." Ynes looked down at her hands and then she gripped the arms of the rocker. "I'd pass the name onto the police. I'd like him to serve time for the murder. I want people to know he's a murderer."

"It's likely the guy has killed more people than your mother. I'm sure he's a known murderer. In some circles anyway."

"I want him to stand trial and be convicted of the crime and go to jail for it."

"Do you know anything about who committed the heist?" Olivia asked. "Do you know who might have carried it out?"

"I was a low-level punk criminal back then." Sewall looked out over the front lawn. A few hydrangeas still bloomed along the fence. "I did some bad stuff. I served time in prison for robbery, assault, selling drugs. I was looking for respect. I didn't get any at home. I don't know if my parents even loved me. Probably not. So I looked for recognition and attention and respect on the street, in the gang. I wanted to be important and I toughened myself up to act the way I needed to, on the outside at least. I was not like that on the inside."

"You left the life of crime?" Ynes asked.

"I left it. I'd had enough of people who only cared about money and power. There were attempts to drag me back in, but I resisted. I got a job. I got two jobs. I saved my money. I bought a house, fixed it up, rented it out. Then I got another one and did the same thing. I have twenty houses and apartment buildings now. I treat people right, my renters, the guys who work for me. You know whose respect I got now? My own." Sewall nodded. "If a person don't have self-respect, then they'll never have it from anyone else. Hard work, doing the right thing, being good to people, staying out of trouble. Those things matter."

"It must have been hard to change the way things were," Olivia said.

"It was damned hard," Sewall said. "You know why I decided to change?"

Ynes shook her head.

"Because of what happened to your mother."

Ynes raised an eyebrow. "Why?"

"I knew the Cooper was going to get hit. The word on the street was the security was so lousy, it was laughable. Someone could waltz right in and make off with millions of dollars' worth of paintings. The kind of art that no one should have on their own walls. Things like that belong to the people, to the world," Sewall said. "I knew when the guys were going to do it, the date and the time. I even knew some of the paintings they were after."

"This was common knowledge?" Ynes asked.

"It was knowledge that *some* people had ... depending on your connections."

"Were you one of the men who carried out the heist?" Ynes asked.

Sewall gave the young woman a look of surprise. "Not me." After a few seconds, the man said, "Have you talked to Tim Mack?"

"We both talked to him at different times," Olivia said.

"And what did you learn?"

"He claims he wasn't involved in the heist."

"Anything else?"

Olivia said, "He was tired of working there, he'd given his notice, he was disgusted with the security problems."

"Do you know he was a musician?"

"Yes."

"Did you know he let other musicians in to jam?

Into the Cooper? Late at night."

"We heard that," Olivia said. "Do you think Tim Mack was in on the heist?"

Sewall made a noise in his throat. "If he was, it was at a very low level. Maybe he knew there would be a break-in, but I doubt he helped take the paintings. He was probably instructed to let the thieves in, not to call the cops, to stay out of the way."

"What would he get if he did those things?" Olivia questioned.

"He was most likely promised some money," Sewall said. "But what he actually got was shot."

"Did the thieves plan to shoot him, do you think?"

"I doubt it. Something didn't go as planned. Only Tim and the robbers know what that was."

"You think Tim knew the thieves?" Ynes asked.

"I can't answer that. It's possible ... one of them, maybe. It's also possible he was in contact with someone else who gave him his instructions."

"So why did you change your life because of my mother?" Ynes asked.

"I heard the woman was shot and killed," Sewall said. "The security at the museum was no good, there were only two guards on duty, unarmed I might add. All the thieves had to do was go in, tie them up, go about their business, get out. Clean, easy. There was no need to shoot those guards. I was sickened by it. The guards were no threat to the robbers. It shouldn't have happened. It was a damned power trip, that's what it was. I'd had enough of those people. I was done. I got out. I wasn't like them. I didn't want to be like them." Sewall paused and rocked slowly for a few moments. "I don't usually talk to people about the past. I agreed to see you for two reasons. One, Mike Reilly helped me out when I decided to change my life and the second reason is because you're the daughter of the woman who got killed. You deserve answers."

"Do you have any guesses who shot my mother?"

"Guesses, yes. Facts, no."

"Can you tell me?"

"If I'm not sure who did it, then I can't tell you. I will not falsely accuse someone."

"The robbers took the security tape of that night," Olivia said.

"I'd hope so," Sewall said. "It would be stupid to leave it behind."

"The security tape of the night before was also taken," Olivia went on.

"I heard that."

"Why would that tape be taken? Did they do a dry run the night before?"

"I don't see them doing that," Sewall said. "They knew their stuff long before the night previous to the heist. There wouldn't be a reason to do a dry run."

"Why take that security tape then?" Olivia questioned.

"Someone besides the robbers might have taken that tape," Sewall said.

"Who?"

"Those are the two questions, who and why. Here's another question ... was Tim Mack working the night before the heist?"

"Yes, he was."

"Maybe you should ask Tim Mack what happened to the tape from the night before the heist."

"We did ask him," Olivia said. "Two separate times."

"Then I'd suggest you ask him again," Sewall said. "Because he was working *both* of those nights."

Ynes asked, "Do you know where the stolen paintings are?"

"They're in Massachusetts. I don't know the exact location. A few hang in private collections, maybe three of them."

"They're all still in Massachusetts?" Ynes asked.

"That's my understanding."

After more discussion about the case with little solid answers forthcoming, Ynes and Olivia thanked Sewall for his help and walked down the porch steps to the walkway.

"One more thing," Sewall said from the porch.

Ynes and Olivia turned back.

"Up in New Hampshire. In Seabrook. You might want to talk to Cindy Wall. Tell her I told you to get in touch. She owns a coffee and lunch place up there, The Hungry Sailor. It might be worth a visit."

25

The Hungry Sailor had closed for the day when Ynes and Olivia met the owner, Cindy Wall, late in the afternoon in Seabrook, New Hampshire. The day was chilly with a strong, cool wind off the ocean and Olivia was grateful for the hot cup of tea Cindy brought to their table at the back of the place.

In her mid-fifties, Cindy was thin and tall with short gray-blond hair framing her face. Her skin had that leathery look from too much sun exposure. The woman had a kind smile, but she seemed nervous about the meeting.

Ynes gave a long explanation about why they had come to see her. "I'm looking into the heist to try and find the name of the person who killed my mother.

Mr. Sewall suggested we talk to you. He didn't say why or what you might have to say."

"Tobey's a good guy. He and I tried to get my brother out of the life for years. My brother, Pete, was in and out of prison his entire adult life. My brother was a good guy, too, he just got mixed up with the wrong crowd and one thing led to another, and he was in with a bad, bad group. Really on the edges of the group, not deeply involved, but still." Cindy let out a long sigh. "Pete was involved in the Cooper heist."

Ynes gasped and her face looked like it might crumble into a million pieces. She put her hands over her face and leaned forward.

As Olivia rubbed her friend's back, she looked to Cindy. "Ynes has never found the name of one of the men who was involved in the robbery. We've never met anyone who admitted to knowing someone who was part of the heist."

Cindy understood. "I don't know a lot of details. My brother kept that to himself, but I do know he wasn't the one who shot your mother."

Ynes brushed at her cheeks and sat up to listen.

"Pete hung out with members of a crime ring. He got mixed up in it. He wanted the money that came with being associated with that group. He told me a few things. Pete found out that the security system at the museum was bad, that it was a place that would be easy to break into."

"How did he know that?" Ynes's voice was hoarse.

"He met some guy through a buddy who told them about the place. Pete got excited about it. He saw dollar signs dancing before his eyes. He wanted to move up in the organization and the heist would place him firmly in one of the top crime groups. Word got back to the boss who was intrigued by the idea and the break-in was organized over a few months.

Pete was one of the guys who got picked to do the dirty work of stealing the paintings. He was told how it would go down and when it would happen. He was told what to take. Everything was planned out. Pete told me they were supposed to go in, tie up the two guards, steal the artwork, and get out. There weren't supposed to be any casualties."

"Did your brother tell you what happened? Why the shooting happened?" Olivia asked.

"No. Pete was closed-mouthed about the details. He never even told me who else was involved."

"Is Pete around?" Ynes asked. "Would he talk to us?"

"Pete died not long ago." Cindy swallowed hard to clear her throat.

Ynes and Olivia offered condolences.

"Pete was found dead in a town outside of Boston with a bullet hole in his head."

The two young women stared at Cindy, their facial muscles tight.

"Pete had been diagnosed with cancer. It was treatable, but it made him realize his mortality. He was afraid that when he died, the other guy involved in the heist would tell the police that Pete killed your mother. Pete never killed anyone. He broke into houses, stole things, sold drugs, beat some people up...." Cindy shook her head. "Believe me, he was no angel, far from it, but he told me he'd never killed anyone and he didn't want to be known as the guy who murdered the woman at the Cooper. Pete was sure he'd be the one who took the blame."

"He didn't tell you who did shoot my mother?" Ynes asked.

"He would never tell me. I don't know who it was. Pete told me there were negotiations going on for the safe return of the paintings to the Cooper. He was sure he'd be fingered as the shooter. I think revealing who killed your mother was part of the bargain. No one would be arrested for the art crime, probably no names would be reported as ones who were responsible for the heist. The news would say an anonymous tip led to the paintings. No reward would be given. But law enforcement wanted the person responsible for the shooting of the two guards. I believe that's the deal being negotiated right now ... the art will be returned to the Cooper with no questions asked, but the police want the guy who killed your mother."

"Pete told you those specifics?" Olivia asked.

"He told me enough that I could piece the things together."

"Someone killed your brother because of the negotiations for the art?" Ynes asked.

"I'd bet my life on it," Cindy said. "Pete sought out a woman who was researching the heist and preparing to write a book about it."

Olivia's stomach turned cold. "Your brother met with her?"

"He did." Cindy nodded. "A day later, Pete was dead."

Ynes covered her mouth with her hand.

"Do you know what Pete told the woman?" Olivia asked.

"Pete wanted it known that he wasn't the shooter. I don't know if he told the researcher the name of the person who was responsible for shooting the guards. He only told me he didn't want to be named as the killer. He was sure his name would be given to the cops as the murderer. Pete said he wasn't serving time for a crime he didn't commit."

"You know that the researcher, the woman your brother talked to, was killed as well?" Olivia asked.

Cindy took in a slow breath. "I saw that on the news."

"Someone didn't want your brother talking, and that person didn't want what he told the researcher to get out." Olivia looked out of the coffee shop window. "Now that your brother is dead, there's nothing to stop him from being named as the shooter."

"Did you tell the police about this?" Ynes asked.

"The police paid me a visit shortly after Pete was killed. I told them what I'm telling you," Cindy said, "but it won't make any difference. There's nothing to stop the negotiations for the art. My brother was silenced. The police can name him as the killer and the artwork can be returned. The real killer can stay free. Case closed."

Ynes groaned.

"Except for one thing." Olivia looked at Ynes and Cindy. "Someone thinks Ynes is getting close to finding out about the heist and is willing to take steps for the information to remain hidden." She told Cindy what had happened to Charles Cohen's housekeeper.

"Is the person responsible for killing Pete and Abigail Millett the same person who wants to keep me from finding out the truth?" Ynes asked.

Something about the mess picked at Olivia, but she couldn't place what was bothering her. She said to Cindy, "The real killer wouldn't want your brother to reveal his identity. The killer would want Pete to be quiet. The person who killed Ynes's mother could have killed your brother and then killed Abigail Millett. But there's something that doesn't fit."

"What is it?" Ynes turned to her friend. "What do you mean?"

Olivia asked Cindy, "Did your brother know a woman named Tilly McIntyre?"

Cindy looked blank. "I don't know the name. Pete never mentioned anyone named Tilly. Who is she?"

Olivia told Cindy that Tilly was Charles Cohen's housekeeper and that the woman had helped to raise Ynes. She addressed her next question to her friend. "Why would someone think Tilly knew anything about the heist? Unless Tilly had connections to thieves and mobsters."

Ynes's mouth opened slightly. "That can't be. I don't think Tilly has any connections to people like that."

"Then who might be afraid that Tilly knows something?" Olivia asked.

Ynes's eyes narrowed in thought and then her expression turned to one of horror. "Charles? My stepfather? You think he's involved?" Ynes's breathing became fast and wheezy. "Oh, no."

"The thought came into my mind," Olivia attempted to minimize her friend's distress. "It doesn't mean it's so. I could be way off base. I'm probably completely wrong."

"I feel sick," Ynes muttered and hurried away to the café's bathroom.

Cindy made eye contact with Olivia. "Don't feel bad. It would make sense that the stepfather might be involved. Maybe the guy wanted to get rid of his wife. If he has money, he could have paid people off to kill her during the heist."

Olivia's stomach began to churn at the idea. She was sorry she'd brought it up. Charles Cohen had been wealthy since he was born. He certainly had the money to pay a thug to murder Ella ... and it probably wasn't that difficult for a man of Charles's means to find some low-life to do it.

A shudder ran down Olivia's back a moment before an incoming text pinged her phone.

It was from Paulina at the leather store.

Randy drew something. You need to see it. Can you come?

26

Ynes was quiet on the drive back to Boston from New Hampshire. After returning the rental car, Ynes decided to go to the condo. She was tired and needed to think, so Olivia took the subway alone to the Fenway area leather shop.

Although Olivia regretted the upset she'd caused Ynes by pointing a finger at Charles Cohen, the idea that he'd had something to do with the heist couldn't be dismissed. The man himself would never have taken part in the actual robbery, but, he could have paid people to break into the museum and steal the paintings. He could also have an association with the mob.

The words Cindy had said pounded in Olivia's

head ... Charles could have had Ella killed in the heist to get rid of her. It was too awful to consider.

Olivia missed home. She'd been talking to Brad every day which only made her more aware of how much she wanted to return to Ogunquit and be surrounded by the people she loved. The case of the stolen art was filled with monstrous characters and unbridled greed that pulled her down and made her feel hopeless and low. Thinking about cooking dinner with Joe, helping Brad in his bookstore, working in the antiques shop, and walking along the beach nearly brought tears to her eyes and made her want to give up on the search for Ella Cohen's killer. But, she would never abandon her friend, especially when Ynes needed her most. Olivia took a deep breath and squared her shoulders.

The early evening darkness shrouded the street and small circles of light from the streetlamps pooled here and there on the empty sidewalk. The leather store looked closed-up and gloomy.

Opening the door to the shop, Olivia saw Paulina standing at the counter looking flustered and distracted. The woman flew from behind the counter, slammed and locked the door, and pulled down the shade. "I'm so glad you're here." Paulina's face was pale and her voice was breathless.

"Randy drew something new?" Olivia asked, slightly unnerved by the woman's demeanor.

"He did. I told him you were going to come by. He's gone upstairs for a minute to the apartment. He'll be back soon." Paulina pushed at a loose strand of hair hanging down from her bun. "I'm worried."

"About the drawing?"

"I'm worried about Randy's safety. If *you* figured out where he works and lives, other people could do the same."

"You think he's in danger? Because of what he saw?"

"Maybe." Paulina wrung her hands together.

"Can I see the drawing or do you want to wait for Randy to come down?"

"I'll show you. I think that's best. You can talk freely to me about it without Randy listening." Paulina hurried to the counter where she removed a sketchpad from the shelf. "Here it is." She flipped the pages and stopped when she found the one she wanted to show Olivia.

Olivia's heart jumped into her throat. "Did Randy communicate anything to you about this picture?"

"I asked if this man was there the day he delivered the box to the townhouse." Paulina's eyes looked moist. "His answer was yes."

"Did he tell you anything more?" Olivia asked.

Paulina shook her head. "I was shocked to see a man in the drawing. All Randy has sketched up until now was Abigail Millett's townhouse by itself. Do you recognize him?"

Olivia peered at the paper with the drawing done in charcoal and a shudder went through her. "I might."

"Is he dangerous?" Paulina searched Olivia's face.

Olivia lifted her eyes to the woman. "I'm not sure."

"Oh, no." Paulina placed her hand over her heart.

Olivia's eyes flicked to the back work room. "Why did Randy go upstairs?"

"He went up to get a tool he left on the kitchen table."

A cold finger of fear suddenly inched over Olivia's skin. "Should he back by now? Why don't we go check on him?"

"You think something...?" A choking sound emanated from the older woman's throat as she rushed into the back room to the staircase that led to the second floor apartment, terrified something might have happened to her son.

Olivia followed close behind and as she passed one of the work stations, she grabbed a small, sharp knife from the tabletop.

Paulina pushed the door open at the top of the stairs. "Randy?" she called as she moved down the hall to the kitchen, to the bedrooms, the bathroom, living room, and dining room. With a wild look in her eyes, she whirled to Olivia and practically wailed. "Where is he?"

"Where does he go when he's worried?" Olivia gripped the knife in her hand. "His room?"

Paulina gave a nod.

Olivia stepped into the young man's bedroom and spoke softly. "Randy? It's Olivia." She had an idea and walked to the closet and slowly opened the door.

Randy sat on the floor with his head in his hands, the ends of shirts and slacks on hangers touching the top of his head.

Olivia knelt down. "Can you come out? Your mom's here. It's okay." She reached her hand out for him and after a moment's hesitation, he grasped it and emerged from his hiding place.

Paulina wrapped her son in a hug and

murmured encouraging words. They went to the dining room and sat down together.

"I showed your picture to Olivia."

Randy looked over at the young woman. The big man gave the impression of a worried and frightened child with his shoulders slumped and his eyes wide.

Paulina brought over one of Randy's communication books.

Olivia asked, "The man in the drawing ... was he nearby on the day you went to Beacon Hill to deliver the box to Abigail Millett?"

Randy touched the "yes" symbol on the first page of his book.

"Are you able to tell me where he was?" Olivia asked.

Randy blinked, walked over to the side table where a pad of paper and a pencil lay, and carried the things back to the dining table where he hunched over drawing feverishly.

Olivia watched as Randy used skilled strokes to expertly draw the Beacon Hill townhouse.

Randy put the pencil down and with his index finger, traced a line along the sidewalk to the front steps of the home.

"He walked down the street and went to the

townhouse," Olivia clarified.

Randy touched the "yes" again.

"Did he walk right in or did he ring the bell?"

Randy mimicked ringing a bell.

"Did Ms. Millett open the door?"

As Randy shook his head, his expression turned hard. He pointed to the front door of the townhouse in his picture and then lifted his arm and made a rotating motion with his hand.

"The man opened the door and went in?" Olivia's heart rate increased.

Randy touched the "yes."

"What happened after that?"

Randy pointed at the clock on the wall.

"You waited. Did the man come out?"

Yes.

"He walked away?"

Yes.

"What did you do after he left?"

Randy used his index and middle finger to make a walking motion along the sidewalk in the drawing, up to the townhouse's door. He looked at Olivia.

"Was the door open or closed?"

Randy put his palms together and then spread them apart.

"It was open," Olivia said.

Suddenly, Randy covered his eyes and his face contorted in anguish.

Olivia looked confused and then Paulina asked her son, "You saw something?"

Randy dropped his hands into his lap.

"Was it blood? In the foyer?" Olivia asked softly.

Randy's index finger pounded the "yes" symbol four times.

"Could you see the woman?"

Randy touched the "no" symbol.

"What did you do next?" Olivia asked.

Randy mimed dropping the box and then he moved his hand quickly from right to left.

His mother asked, "You dropped the box and ran away?"

Randy gave a little nod.

"Did the man see you?" Olivia questioned.

Randy's shoulders raised and lowered in a shrug.

"Were there any other people on the street or sidewalk when you were there?"

Randy touched the "no" symbol.

Olivia told Randy that she had talked to this man at a hotel in Boston. "He wanted me to give my friend's suitcase to him. I got a bad vibe from the man so I didn't give him what he asked for. He told me his name was Michael White, but I'm sure he was lying. If you ever see him again, you must tell your mother right away. I think it would be helpful if you and your mom take your drawing of the man to the police so she can report what you saw at the townhouse."

Randy shrunk in his seat.

"Can you do that?" Olivia asked with a gentle tone.

Randy lifted his eyes to the young woman and gave a tiny nod.

Olivia smiled. "Thank you, Randy. Thank you for drawing the man. It helps me a lot."

BEFORE LEAVING THE LEATHER SHOP, Olivia used her phone to take a photo of Randy's drawing of Michael White at the townhouse. Now, she walked along Boylston Street thinking back on the night after the baseball game when she strolled with Brad on this same sidewalk and received the text from Ynes telling her she needed help. The details of what they'd learned since that evening now swirled in her head and made her dizzy.

Abigail Millett was already dead before Michael White arrived at the townhouse and went in. Her door was unlocked and open when White got there. Who killed her? What did the woman know that led to her murder? Did Michael White know Ms. Millett had some incriminating information in her possession? Is that why he was at her house? Did Michael White take part in the heist twenty years ago? What about Ynes's stepfather, Charles Cohen? Did he have something to do with the heist? Did he want Ella killed?

Olivia rubbed her at forehead, the beginnings of a headache pinching at her temples.

Someone felt threatened by Abigail Millett's research and by Ynes trying to find her mother's killer. But, why now? Plenty of people had researched the heist over the past twenty years. What was different now that made someone feel so backed into a corner that Abigail Millett was murdered, Pete Wall was killed, and Tilly was attacked? What new thing had come to light?

The museum security tape from the night *before* the heist had been popping into Olivia's brain for days. Why was that tape taken? What was on it? What happened in the museum on that night that had to remain hidden?

Those musicians had been jamming in the museum again and the police showed up and kicked them out. So what? The same thing had happened on other nights. What was different that made someone steal the security tape?

Tim Mack. Olivia had to talk to Tim Mack again.

Another idea flashed in Olivia's mind. Who was on duty with Tim the night before the heist and what would that person have to say about that evening?

27

A fter sifting through news articles, reports, and documents, Ynes finally found the name of the man who was on duty with Tim Mack the night before the heist. In his seventies, Benny Goldman was living in West Roxbury and agreed to meet with Ynes and Olivia at his home.

Goldman's place was a white, two-story dwelling with black shutters located in the neat, well-tended neighborhood of smaller, middle-class houses. Pots of colorful flowers and pumpkins lined the steps to the front door.

The living room was decorated for Halloween with figurines of black cats on the bookshelf, several glass pumpkins on the mantel, and a dish of candy corn sitting on the coffee table.

"Our grandkids love the decorations." Goldman winked. "My wife and I enjoy them, too." The man had silver hair, warm brown eyes, and broad shoulders. "Please have a seat. What can I do to help?"

Olivia liked Goldman right away. "We wondered if you could remember anything about the night before the heist took place at the Cooper."

"It's been almost twenty years ... hard to believe." Goldman shook his head. "I remember the shift. It stuck in my brain cells because the police talked to me several times about it. I was glad I hadn't been scheduled to work the next night. I would hate to have that hanging over me. What can I tell you? What would you like to know?"

"Was it a regular shift?" Olivia asked. "Did anything out of the ordinary happen?"

"It was pretty much a regular night, although the police came in to kick out the jammers. You know about the musicians who used to practice in the Cooper sometimes?"

Ynes said, "We've read about it."

"Your brother joined in a few times," Goldman said to Ynes.

"Stepbrother," Ynes told him. "I've heard Erik hung around with those guys."

"Yeah, so a group of them would come some

nights to the museum and jam together," Goldman said. "It was completely against the rules. It didn't happen often ... it wasn't every night or anything. Maybe once or twice a month. Tim Mack, the other guard, was a musician. He knew some of the guys. He let them in."

"Did you object?" Olivia asked.

Goldman gave a shrug. "I knew it was wrong. I didn't see the harm in it though. It didn't bother me. The first time, I told Tim I didn't think it was a good idea, but he blew me off so I didn't bring it up again. I enjoyed listening to the music. It broke up the night, made the time go by faster. Those guys drank and took some drugs while they were there. I was against it. I didn't involve myself with that stuff. I drew the line at that. I was working. I wasn't going to get drunk or high or whatever."

"Did Tim drink when the guys were there?" Ynes asked.

"Yeah, he did. I figured if anything happened, at least I was sober. Nothing ever happened anyway, nothing serious." Goldman's face clouded and he said softly, "Until the next night." He looked at Ynes and sighed. "Your mother was a fine person, young lady. Smart, nice, took her job seriously. I don't know first-hand what happened that night, but I do know Ella would have done her best."

Ynes gave a nod of thanks for the man's kind comments.

"Did anything else happen the night before besides the musicians being there?" Olivia asked.

"Just the police coming in. The museum director had enough of the guys using the museum as their personal practice studio and asked the cops to come by and check on the place now and then. They'd be more cars parked outside when the guys showed up. It would tipoff the police that a jam session was probably going on. The night before the heist, the police told the group they'd be arrested next time and if they didn't want a record, they better knock off sneaking into the Cooper. The cops were angry about having to come by and kick them out. They didn't need the extra work. They almost arrested some of the guys that night. I don't know why they didn't."

"How did they treat you and Tim? The police had to know one of you let the musicians in."

"They knew it was Tim. They left me alone except to tell me I'd better start doing my job. They were right, of course."

"Was Tim drunk that night?" Ynes asked.

"He was feeling it, yeah."

"Did you know the security tape from the night before the heist had been removed from the museum?" Olivia questioned.

"I read that somewhere," Goldman said. "I never learned officially why it was taken or who took it."

"Officially?" Olivia narrowed her eyes.

"Well." Goldman shifted around in his chair. "I sort of had an idea what might have happened to it."

"You did?" Olivia had to hold herself back from leaping off the sofa in excitement.

"I could be wrong. Maybe the thieves took both evenings' security tapes on the night of the heist."

"But what were your suspicions?" Olivia leaned a little forward.

"I had the notion Tim Mack might have taken it."

Surprise washed over Olivia's face. "Why would he?"

"Tim's younger brother was there that night. Adam. He was a bass player. Adam was friendly with your stepbrother," he told Ynes.

"Why would it matter that Adam was there?" Ynes asked. "Why would that make Tim take the tape?"

"Adam had been arrested a couple of times for selling drugs. He had used pretty heavily in the past, too. It was the first time Adam had shown up to jam. I remember Tim wasn't too happy about him being there. Anyway, when I let the cops in from the panel on the security desk, I hustled to tell Tim they were coming. While the other guys scurried around throwing beer bottles out, putting the instruments away, Tim hauled his brother out of the gallery and to an exit at the side of the building. He didn't want the cops to see Adam because the kid was on probation. I recall your stepbrother high-tailed it away with them. I'd bet he didn't want to get arrested and have your stepfather find out."

"So you think Tim Mack took the security tape from that night so the police wouldn't find out his brother was there?" Olivia asked.

"That's what I think," Goldman said.

"How old was Adam?" Ynes asked.

"Not sure. He was younger than the other guys. He was more your stepbrother's age."

"Did you confront Tim and ask if he took the tape?" Olivia questioned.

"Nah. I visited Tim in the hospital a couple of times. I didn't know then that the security tape was missing. Tim never came back to work. I think I saw him maybe once after that. I ran into him in town. Somebody told me he moved away." Goldman shook his head. "I heard Tim got hounded pretty bad by the press. A lot of people thought Tim had to be in on the heist. I don't know about that. For a little while, I wondered if he had been involved in the robbery one way or another, but I changed my mind. I don't think he was. It didn't seem to fit with the guy I knew. Who knows though? People can do some crazy things ... things you don't expect from them."

Unease fluttered in Olivia's veins. Was Tim involved in the heist? "Did you have any suspects in mind? Was there someone you were suspicious of? Someone you thought might have set up the robbery or been involved in some way?"

"Everybody talked back then," Goldman said. "It was this person ... it was that gang. The art was stolen because some thug used to go there as a kid to get out of the cold and fell in love with some of the paintings and decided to take them. Really? Who knows? I suppose the police know things. It would sure be nice to have them returned. I'd rush right down there to see them again." Goldman's eyes grew sad. "It wasn't right. They didn't have to shoot the guards. Neither one was armed. We never carried any weapons. They must have known that."

"You knew the museum's security was lacking?" Olivia asked.

"I knew, sure. Even so, I never thought anybody would try to rob the place. It just didn't seem possible. Tim was always griping about the security. I listened to his complaints, but I thought he was blowing it out of proportion." He shook his head. "See what I knew."

"What ever happened to Tim's brother, Adam?" Ynes asked.

"I heard Adam turned himself around and became a physician's assistant. He works at a hospital in Boston. He's done well for himself."

"Maybe his brother's watchful eye made the difference and he decided to make a change for the better," Olivia speculated as she reached into her bag and took out her phone. "Do you recognize this man?" She showed Goldman the photo she'd taken of Randy's drawing of Michael White.

Goldman put his glasses on and held the phone up. "At first I thought the face might be familiar, but I guess not." He handed the phone back to Olivia. "I don't believe I know him. Who is he?"

"I don't know. He says his name is Michael White."

"You don't think that's his real name?"

"I don't."

"What's he done? Is he in trouble?" Goldman asked.

"I think he's done some really bad things," Olivia said.

Goldman's eyes went wide. "Well, you best stay clear of him then."

A cold chill of anxiety rolled over Olivia's skin. "That's probably a very good idea."

28

Olivia knocked at the first floor apartment in Medford and Tim Mack opened the door. "Thanks for seeing me," she told him.

Olivia had called Mack's cell phone in the hopes that the man hadn't changed the number when he moved from outside of D.C. back to the Boston area.

Mack led her inside, down the hall, through the kitchen, to a sunroom at the back of the house. Light streamed in through the big windows on three sides of the room making the space pleasantly warm and comfortable.

"I thought I'd be seeing you again," Mack said. His face didn't register any joy at seeing Olivia.

"Why did you think that?"

"I could see you were persistent. I didn't think

you'd give up looking for answers." Mack looked tired. "Did you find the name of the man who killed Ella Cohen?"

"No."

Mack raised an eyebrow in surprise. "I thought you'd have figured everything out by now."

"We haven't."

Neither one said anything for a few moments.

"I understand your brother is doing well." Olivia held Mack's eyes.

Mack sighed. "Who gave you that bit of news?"

"One of your former partners at the Cooper. Benny Goldman."

Mack looked out one of the windows. "I thought you'd talk to Benny eventually."

"Did you take the security tape from the museum that night? Because your brother was there?" Olivia asked.

Mack ran his hand over the top of his head. "I won't ever admit to doing that if the police ask me."

"I'll take that as a *yes*. Do you still have it?"

"No. It doesn't exist anymore."

"You took it so no one would know your brother was violating the terms of his probation?"

"If you say so." Mack still trained his gaze out the window.

Olivia said, "Mr. Mack, I'm not taping this conversation. I'm only looking to find the name of the man who killed Ella Cohen. I don't care about the other stuff. Not much anyway."

"When the cops came, I showed my brother out the side door of the museum."

"Erik Cohen was there, too?"

Mack turned to Olivia. "I didn't care about him. He followed us as I dragged my brother out of the place."

"Something is bothering me about the timing," Olivia said.

"Meaning what? The timing of what?" Mack asked.

"Your group was jamming, the cops came, you got your brother out of the museum, you took the security tape. It seems kind of drastic ... to take the tape, I mean. What were you really trying to hide your brother from?"

Mack narrowed his eyes. "I don't know what you mean."

"Did you know the Cooper was going to be hit the next night?"

"No."

"I think you did. I think you were afraid the cops would be asking a lot of questions if they got hold of the security tape from the night before the heist and saw that your brother was in the museum."

Mack bit the inside of his cheek. "Why would that matter?"

"It might matter if your brother knew about the heist. Maybe he was involved in it?" Olivia speculated, waiting for Mack's reaction. She could see the man's breathing rate increase.

"Your brother *did* know about the heist. Otherwise, why would you bother taking the security tape? Why would it even occur to you to take it?" Olivia used a gentle tone. "I'm not trying to get your brother in trouble. I'm not going to share the information with anyone. I just want to know the name of the shooter."

"Does Benny Goldman think I took the tape because my brother was involved in the heist?" Mack eyed Olivia.

"Absolutely not. He thinks you took it because your brother was on probation."

Mack leaned forward, his elbows on his knees, his head in his hands. "Adam knew about the heist. He and some other guy had spread the information about the Cooper being an easy mark. He didn't do it looking for someone to break-in. He was just shooting his mouth off in some bar, somebody heard him and asked questions. The news got around. A guy named Pete Wall convinced my brother to tell him what he'd heard about the security systems. I'd blabbed that stuff to Adam in one of my rants about the museum. Pete Wall wanted Adam to take part in the heist. Adam was a loose cannon back then. He got all excited about joining this ring of thugs, about making all kinds of money from the heist. No way was I letting him go down that road. I told Adam I'd go to the cops and tell them everything unless he dropped the idea of taking part. He was furious. I told him I'd tell his probation officer. He finally backed down. But the heist was going to take place with or without him, and if I didn't do what they expected me to do, then Adam would suffer the consequences."

"Did Adam know when the hit was going to take place?"

"Yeah, he told me when." Mack swallowed hard.

"Did he tell you anything else about the plan?" Olivia asked.

"Adam told me that two guys would be at the side door at a certain time that night. I was to let them in. The men would tie up me and the other guard and then they would go to a specific gallery and steal two paintings. Then they would leave." Mack's face had lost all of its color. "That's not how it happened."

"What did happen?"

"It happened like I told you before. Those cops showed up and demanded to be let inside. I thought it might have had something to do with the alarms going off earlier ... or I wondered if they knew a hit was planned. I started to panic. I was afraid the two robbers were going to show up any minute expecting me to let them in at the side door. I didn't know what to do. The cops were yelling at me to let them in. Finally, I hit the button on the panel of the security desk to allow them inside."

"You thought they were real cops, but they were the robbers," Olivia said. "They didn't go to the side door. They went to the back entrance. Nobody told you the robbers would be dressed as cops."

Mack nodded. "When I wasn't at the side door like I was supposed to be, I thought the robbers would come around to the back. I thought the cops would see them and realize I was supposed to let them in. I panicked. My brain froze up. I didn't know what to do. The rest all happened like I told you before." Mack's voice choked out his words. "If I'd handled it better, Ella wouldn't have been shot. She died because I didn't know what to do."

"That's not true," Olivia told him. "It wasn't your fault. Those monsters threatened your brother if you didn't do what they asked. Ella died because those robbers had no respect for life. They shot her for no reason. They shot you for no reason. It was their fault. All of it was their fault."

"Are you going to tell the police?" Mack's voice cracked.

"There's no reason to. It wouldn't help the case if I told them," Olivia said. "The only person I'm going to tell is Ella's daughter, and she won't tell the police either."

Mack wiped at his eyes. "Thank you."

"Did you know the robbers?" Olivia asked. "Do you know who they are?"

"I never saw them before."

Do you know which one shot Ella?"

"I know. I remember his face. If I ever saw him again, I'd know him."

Olivia pulled her phone out and handed it to Mack. "Look at this drawing of a man. Do you recognize him?"

Mack gingerly took the phone and looked at Randy's drawing of Michael White. "I don't know him. It's not the same man who shot Ella."

"He'd be twenty years younger than he is in this

picture," Olivia said. "Can you imagine him as a younger man? Would he seem familiar then?"

Mack shook his head. "I don't remember seeing his face."

"All we want is the name of the shooter. Why is that so hard?" Olivia shoved her phone back into her bag. "You know Pete Wall is dead? The man who got your brother to tell him about the Cooper's security system. He was shot to death."

"I know." Mack met Olivia's eyes.

"He went to talk to the woman who was researching the Cooper heist. He was killed the next day," Olivia told him.

Mack sat up straight. "I knew he was dead. I didn't know he'd talked to the researcher."

"Why did you come back to Boston?" Olivia asked.

"To make sure my brother stays safe. Pete Wall was killed. The researcher was killed. Is my brother in danger for knowing things about the heist? Is someone going after anyone who might know some things?" Mack looked at Olivia with a grave expression. "You'd better give up on this case. Go home. Tell Ella's daughter to leave it alone."

"I don't think she will."

"Why not? It's a fool's errand."

A rush of adrenaline ran through Olivia's body. "I think it's too late for that. I think we know too many things, even though not enough of it adds up. I also think we'd better figure it out soon before somebody thinks we know more than we do."

29

D enise Millett Spencer, Abigail's daughter, phoned Ynes to tell her she wasn't able to find her mother's most recent notebook. She invited Olivia and Ynes to the townhouse to look around and they agreed on a time to meet.

Walking up the narrow road on Beacon Hill to Ms. Millett's former home, Ynes glanced around. "It's a bad feeling knowing someone was killed in that house."

Olivia eyed the place thinking about the first time she'd arrived at the brick townhouse with Brad and discovered the door open and the blood in the foyer. "It's even worse not knowing exactly why she was killed."

Olivia rang the bell and within a minute, Denise welcomed them inside.

"Most of the furniture has been moved out and the house has been put on the market," Denise told them. "I could never live here so I listed the place with a Realtor. I hate to see it go, but...." She lifted her arms in a helpless shrug. "I can barely stand to be in here for a few minutes."

Denise led Ynes and Olivia to Abigail's office, a good-sized room with two walls of bookshelves, high ceilings, and wide windows looking out over a small, brick patio. The large wooden desk was the only piece of furniture left in the room.

"This was my mother's office. She always left her notebook on the desk when she was working. I haven't been able to find it." Denise opened a door to a walk-in closet. A large safe sat on the floor, its door open. "My mother kept her laptop and notebooks in here along with documents important to what she was working on. The most recent notebook found in here was dated six weeks ago. The one she'd been working in is missing."

"The intruder probably took it," Olivia said as she looked around the room.

"I agree," Denise said. She removed a notebook and took it to the desk. "There's a note in here at the back that mentions Pete Wall. Mr. Wall contacted my mother and they set a date and time to meet here at the house. My mother was killed two days later." Denise slid the opened notebook closer to Ynes and Olivia so they could see.

As the young women read the entry, Denise said, "There are some notes about Pete Wall in there, his crime history, his incarceration history, his possible ties to the Cooper Museum heist. My mother made a note that the man told her on the phone that he was one of the robbers of the Cooper and that he could tell her who else was involved, how the heist was planned, and how it was carried out."

Olivia looked over at Denise. "Your mother must have had a wealth of information taken down in her notebook from her meeting with Pete Wall."

"It seems the intruder helped himself to that book," Denise said with a hard edge to her voice. "I've personally gone over every inch of this room trying to find it. It's not here."

Ynes ran her hand over the top of the desk. "Someone killed your mother because Pete Wall talked to her, and Pete Wall was killed because he talked. The man was supposed to take the information to his grave, not share it with anyone else. He paid the price for not staying silent."

J. A. WHITING

"And my mother paid the price for listening to him." Denise crossed her arms over her chest and let her eyes move around the room.

"Did your mother use a briefcase?" Olivia asked.

"She did. It's in the closet. It's empty except for a few pens and a pad of paper with nothing written on it. I was careful with the things in this room and with those in her bedroom when they were packed away. I was careful with every room, but especially so with the two. That notebook is gone." Denise released a long sigh. "Would you like to walk through the house? I can give you a tour. I don't know if it would be helpful?"

Ynes and Olivia agreed and were led through the historical townhouse's many rooms. The craftsmanship of the place was impressive with beautiful details in every one of the spaces.

Denise paused at the entrance to the sitting room off the foyer, the muscles in her jaw tensing. "My mother was found in there. Blood was found here in the foyer so the attack must have started as soon as my mother opened the door. She must have broken away from the intruder and run into the sitting room." The woman shook her head. "You can see why I couldn't live here. I can't stand the thoughts of what happened in these rooms."

Olivia knew the feeling all too well. She couldn't walk past the house in Maine where she'd been held by her aunt's murderer without having a near panic attack.

After leaving the townhouse, Ynes and Olivia walked through the darkening Common without speaking, each one lost in their thoughts about Abigail Millett, Pete Wall, and who wanted them dead.

The scuff of a shoe on the path was heard close behind them and Ynes wheeled around, her arms raised up to her chest, ready to fight.

"Take it easy." A man wearing a winter hat, a dark jacket, jeans, and a pair of sunglasses despite the lack of sunlight, stood arms-length from the young women. "I've got a message for you."

"Who are you?" Olivia used a low, demanding tone to hide her fright.

"It doesn't matter who I am." The guy kept his voice down. "Here's your message. I'll only say it once. The guy you want is Ricky Spence."

"What does the mean?" Olivia asked.

"Don't interrupt," the guy told her gruffly. "Spence killed Pete Wall and the Millett woman." The dark figure looked at Ynes. "Spence also killed your mother."

Ynes gasped and took a step back.

"Here's his address." The guy rattled off a street name, a number, and an apartment number.

"Why are you telling us this?" Olivia demanded, full of distrust of the man.

"I'm giving you a message. The information is from Jimmy Farber. He says he'll deny ever telling you anything if the police ask him about it."

"Why would Farber give us this information?" Olivia could feel a dribble of nervous sweat on the back of her neck.

"Pete Wall was an associate of Mr. Farber. Someone overstepped his bounds by killing him." The man adjusted his sunglasses. "That someone was Ricky Spence." Without another word, the guy turned on his heel and disappeared into the shadows that were gathering on the Common.

Olivia looked at her friend and touched Ynes's arm.

"Is he lying?" Ynes whispered.

"It didn't seem like it." Olivia looked over her shoulder in the direction the man had gone.

"Ricky Spence." Ynes's hands clenched into fists and her jaw set. Her chest rose and fell rapidly with each breath. "Let's go to that address."

"Why would we do that?" Olivia asked, a touch of panic in her voice.

Ynes's words came out in a whisper. "I want to see the man who killed my mother."

"Not now. Let's think about this. What are you going to do? Ring his bell? Knock on his door? And then what?"

"I just want to see his face. I'm not going to do anything."

"Do you have a knife in your bag?" Olivia asked.

"No. Check it if you want." Ynes held the bag out.

"You can't attack this guy," Olivia warned. "You can't do anything to him. You can't be a vigilante."

Ynes's expression was as hard as cement. "I just want to see his face. Don't come if you don't want to."

Olivia groaned. "If you try anything, I swear I'll call the police on you. You aren't going to ruin your life over this guy." Olivia knew it was a stupid thing to say to someone whose mother's life was ruined by this guy, but she couldn't think of anything else. "Ynes?"

"I heard you." Ynes had used her phone to pull up a map with Spence's address.

"You're just going to look at him?" Olivia asked. "Nothing else?"

Ynes's dark eyes bored into Olivia's. "I'm just

going to look at him."

The dark-haired young woman took off down the hill to Arlington Street, with her friend trotting after her.

Ricky Spence lived in an expensive, three-story townhouse on a trendy street in the South End. Ynes and Olivia stood in front of a small restaurant diagonally across the street from the man's place. Lots of people walked along both sides of the street, returning from work, or heading out for dinner or to shop, or to go to the gym. Olivia wished she was one of them.

"He lives well, doesn't he?" Ynes asked.

Olivia eyed Ynes trying to gauge her mind-set. "Should we come back another time? After you've had time to process this?"

"I've had years to process this." Ynes stared at the townhouse.

"What are you planning to do?" Before Ynes could answer, Olivia spotted the silhouettes of two men moving in front of one of the windows of Spence's place. "There's more than one person in there."

"Let's ring the doorbell."

"What are you going to say when someone answers?" Olivia asked.

"I'll ask for Richard Spence."

"And then?"

"I'll look him in the eye ... and then I'll tell him I have the wrong address. I'll tell him he isn't the Ricky Spence I'm looking for ... and then we'll leave."

"What if he knows who you are? What if he recognizes you?"

"We won't go inside. We'll stay on the landing."

"Put your hair up," Olivia said. "Do you have those fake eyeglasses in your bag? Put them on. Alter your appearance a little."

"It'll be okay. He isn't going to do anything to us."

"Why wouldn't he?" Olivia's voice rose an octave. "He's killed at least two people. Can't we come back? You can wear your wig. I'll put a scarf on my head."

Movement at the townhouse caught Ynes's eye. "Someone's coming out. It might be Spence."

Olivia turned to look and she almost choked. She grabbed Ynes's arm and spun her around to face the restaurant. "It's Michael White." The words caught in her throat. "Michael White just left Spence's place."

"hy would White be in Spence's house?" Ynes asked. "Are you sure it was him?"

"I'm positive." Olivia tried to slow her breathing. "Maybe they work together."

"Is he out of sight?"

Taking a quick look over her shoulder, Olivia said, "He's gone."

"Let's go then."

"Back to the condo?" Olivia hoped.

"To Spence's place." Ynes crossed the street with her friend right behind her and they climbed the granite steps to Spence's front door.

"Be ready to run," Olivia suggested as Ynes rang the bell.

They waited two minutes and then Ynes pushed the button again.

Still no one came.

"Maybe Spence went out the back door," Olivia said.

Ynes pounded on the door.

"He's not going to answer. We can come back another time." Olivia walked down the steps to the sidewalk and Ynes reluctantly followed.

"Wait. Let's go around to the back. There must be a back door. Maybe the bell doesn't work," Ynes said.

"I heard the bell ring," Olivia told her. "He isn't in there, or he doesn't want to be bothered."

"I'm going to check." Ynes walked around the block to the back driveway that led behind the building. A four-car garage stood near the rear property line. A walkway led to the back doors of the townhouses. A small deck ran along the back of each home.

"Great," Olivia sighed when she saw there was a rear door to Spence's place.

Ynes rang the rear bell, but no one answered.

Sliding glass doors led from the interior of the townhouse to the deck and light spilled out from whatever room those doors opened to.

Ynes glanced at Olivia and then walked along the deck to knock on the glass doors. Just as she raised her arm, Ynes held her hand in mid-air and called to her friend. "Liv. Come here."

Olivia hesitated, not liking the sound of Ynes's voice.

"Liv."

Olivia moved to Ynes's side. "What is it?" She looked through the glass door into the townhouse's living room and gasped. "Oh, hell."

Spence was on his back on the floor. His throat cut. Blood pooling next to him.

Olivia turned and grabbed Ynes's arm just as the young woman slid slowly to the floor of the deck in a faint.

"Oh, heck," Olivia muttered, kneeling next to her friend. "We need to get out of here. Ynes."

In a minute, Ynes's eyes fluttered and opened. Olivia helped her to sit up. "Can you stand? Do you need to rest a bit first?"

Ynes took a quick look through the glass doors, groaned, and clutched her stomach. "Help me up. Let's go. I'm so dizzy."

Olivia held tight to Ynes's arm, guiding the wobbly young woman back to the front of the building and across the street where she flagged a cab to take them back to the condo.

~

YNES STRETCHED out on the sofa with her eyes closed while Olivia paced up and down the room.

"Michael White killed Ricky Spence." Olivia talked out loud trying to make sense of the case details. "Why? Is White working for Jimmy Faber? Were Michael White and Ricky Spence in rival gangs? Spence must have been killed in retaliation … because Spence killed Pete Wall. It's all too confusing." Olivia kept pacing. "We should have called 911. But what would it have mattered? Spence was dead. He lost too much blood."

With a blank expression, Ynes pushed herself up to sitting position and rubbed at her temples. "Spence. I finally know the name of the man who killed my mother. After all this time, now I know." She looked up at Olivia. "But, it doesn't make me feel any better." A tear escaped from Ynes's eye. "It makes me feel worse. You were right. It doesn't matter. I thought I was helping my mother by finding him, but it doesn't matter. It doesn't help anything."

Olivia hurried over and sat next to her friend,

her arm around Ynes's shoulders. "The man is dead. He can't hurt anyone else. After time passes, it will be a comfort to know that."

Ynes picked up the pillow from the sofa, folded it in half, placed it on her knees, and let her head rest against it. "Seeing the blood, seeing him dead, made me think of something. Images came into my head. Images from when I was a little girl."

"What images?"

"Erik and Charles arguing ... in the living room of the townhouse we used to live in. Erik was sweating. Charles was so angry," Ynes said without lifting her head. "I think I saw blood on Erik's shirt. It was the night my mother died."

"Are these new images?" Olivia asked, rubbing her friend's back.

"I think they've been in my head all this time, but I see them more clearly now." Ynes turned her head and looked at Olivia. "Why would he have blood on his shirt?"

"Your stepfather slapped him that night. Maybe Erik got a bloody nose?"

"I feel so dizzy," Ynes said. "I think I remember getting up that night. I think I heard Erik when he came home. I stood near my bedroom door, listening."

"Did you hear something?"

"Erik looked kind of wild and messy," Ynes said. "He told me to go back to bed. His voice was mean. He called me *punk*. *Go back to bed, you little bitch. Just like your mother.* That's what I think he said. I think he swore at me."

"He was like that with you, wasn't he? He was about thirteen years older. He probably didn't want anything to do with you."

"You're right, he never wanted anything to do with me. Why are these memories popping up? Why now?" Ynes asked.

Olivia said, "You've just seen your stepfather and stepbrother after a long while apart. Seeing them brings things to the forefront, things you haven't thought of in a long time. It's also been a very stressful week and a half."

Ynes sat up and pressed her back against the sofa. "Something seems off. I feel like there's something I'm missing."

"Why don't you go to sleep. Your brain needs a rest."

"Not yet. Talk to me. Look up Michael White. See if anything comes up about him," Ynes requested.

"I think he's using a false name, but I'll have a look." Olivia got her laptop and began to search.

"There are millions of men with that name. When I put in *Boston*, along with his name, it narrows it down, but there are hundreds of men that come up."

"Who is he?" Ynes asked. "He came looking for my bag at the hotel. He tried to get you to give it to him. How did he know you had my bag? How did he know I was at that hotel?"

"These criminals seem to be able to find out a lot of things," Olivia sighed. "They must have a network. They must share information." Turning quickly to Ynes, she asked, "Who knew you were coming here from D.C.?"

"Charles knew. You knew. Abigail Millett knew. I think Tim Mack knew. I think it came up when I talked to him in D.C. months ago."

"Charles knew," Olivia repeated. "Would he have told Tilly you were coming to town?"

"Yeah, I think he would have."

"What about Erik? Would Charles tell him?"

"I'm pretty sure he would."

Olivia said, "So there are more people who knew you were coming than you thought. And those people might have told other people. Tilly would have told her husband. Charles might have shared the information with a friend or an associate. Erik might have mentioned it to someone. The web grows larger. And someone in that web must know Michael White."

Ynes shuddered. "Things are escalating. A number of people have been killed. Michael White knows what you look like. He came looking for my bag, so he, or whoever sent him, knows I have information about the heist. Tilly was attacked. Pete Wall and Abigail Millet were murdered by Ricky Spence. Michael White killed Ricky Spence." Ynes got to her feet, her eyes full of fear. "Why hasn't someone come for me?"

"Maybe whoever is in charge doesn't think you know anything incriminating," Olivia said with a calm tone, but her insides were roiling.

"They think I don't know anything, but Tilly does?" Ynes stared at her friend for a few moments before hurrying away to her bedroom. "Pack your bag. Those thugs know where we are. Who knows when they'll decide to come for us. Let's get out of here. Now."

Olivia jumped to her feet. "Where will we go? To a hotel?"

"To a place with better security. To my stepfather's house in Weston."

For a second, a sense of apprehension washed

over Olivia and a thought moved through her mind, but she didn't voice it.

Is staying with your stepfather a good idea?

She shook off the momentary worry and headed to her room to pack her bag, thinking there might very well be an additional reason for Ynes's suggestion.

31

Charles Cohen owned an estate in Weston about twenty minutes outside of Boston. He had the townhouse in the city for a matter of convenience, for late nights in the office or when attending an event that lasted into the wee hours, but the mansion was considered his primary residence, the place he spent most of his time outside of his office.

The twenty-five-thousand-square-foot Federal Baroque colonial manor situated on over four acres abutting conservation land had twenty-four rooms, nine full bathrooms, five half bathrooms, a music room, game room, tea room, wine cellar, two floating-style staircases, a ten-car garage, and a wine cellar. There were sweeping lawns, a heated swimming pool, tennis courts, fire pits, an outdoor kitchen, waterfalls, and a gated entry. A four-thou-sand square foot guest house with four bedrooms and four and a half baths sat snug among mature trees in a private location on the property.

The cab dropped the young women at the gate house where Ynes inserted a small card into a metal mailbox-type thing. The iron gate slid quietly open.

"Charles doesn't like cabs driving up to the house unless there's a lot of luggage to carry," Ynes explained. "Usually, there's a guard in the gate house. We could call for a golf cart to come pick us up, but it's not far."

"A guard? A golf cart to pick you up?" Olivia eyed her friend.

After walking around a bend in the driveway, the mansion came into view and Olivia stopped in her tracks with her mouth hanging open. "You're kidding."

Surrounded by impeccable landscaping and carefully placed lighting to highlight the architec-ture and the grounds, the massive brick and stone structure had a portico and large porches spreading out on both sides.

Ynes gave her friend a little smile. "Charles thinks the covered porches on the front make the house less imposing."

"Tell me again. What exactly does Charles do for a living?" Olivia teased making Ynes chuckle. "I thought the townhouse in Boston was outrageous. You grew up here?"

"Charles bought the place when I was about ten. It scared me. It was too big, too many rooms, too imposing. Tilly understood a little kid's fears and made sure my room was nice and cozy for me. I liked the townhouse in the city better."

A short, older woman opened the door to greet them and Ynes introduced Greta, another housekeeper, to Olivia. Greta told them that she'd set out snacks in the kitchen for them, made some small talk, and then disappeared.

When Ynes showed her friend to her room, Olivia's eyes popped. "People live like this?"

Ynes bopped her on the arm. "My room's right next door."

The two sat in comfortable chairs in front of the fireplace in Olivia's room.

"Why didn't you come here when you came to the city instead of going to the hotel and renting the short-term condo?" Olivia asked.

"I don't feel comfortable here. I don't know who I can trust. I can't control the environment in the house. There are too many people working here, too many people coming and going. There's too much space. I'm feeling panicky after seeing Ricky Spence dead. I thought we could stay tonight and then leave in the morning and go someplace else. I don't like anyone knowing where I'm staying. Like you said, if I tell Charles or Tilly something, they might mention it to someone else, and then pretty soon, a whole bunch of people know."

Ynes went on. "Charles is in the city until later this evening. He wants to have a late drink with us when he gets back. He told me Erik is staying in the carriage house for a few days. A pipe burst in his condo and the place is being redone. He'll probably join us for drinks."

Olivia nodded.

Ynes sighed. "Just one big, happy family."

Olivia looked Ynes in the eye. "Did you have another reason, besides our safety, for coming here tonight?"

"Yes."

"What is it?" Olivia had a pretty good idea what the answer would be.

"I thought we could have a look around Charles's home office while he is still in the city." Ynes's jaw set. "We're both suspicious of Charles. Is there a possibility he was involved in the Cooper heist in some way? Does he have *business* associates he made a deal with? Associates who he might have arranged the heist and split the profits with? Is Charles in some way responsible for my mother's death?"

"What if we get caught in Charles's office?" Olivia asked.

"Then we'll make up a story." Ynes stood.

"It will have to be a good one."

"Shall we?" Ynes headed for the door.

"No time like the present," Olivia groaned.

Ynes led the way to Charles's office on the first floor. None of the help was around, so she opened the door and softly closed it behind them. And then she turned the lock. "We don't want anyone barging in on us."

Olivia admired the beautiful wood on the walls, the bookshelves, the arched windows that looked out onto the lawn. Moonlight came in through the window and pooled on the expensive area rug near the massive desk.

"Charles has file cabinets and a safe behind these doors. You want to start looking in the desk drawers while I see if I can get the safe open? He always alternates between three different combinations of numbers. Let's hope he hasn't changed to something new."

Olivia sat gingerly in Charles Cohen's leather desk chair and opened one of the drawers. About thirty to forty hanging folders lined the drawer. She reached for one of them to start the search for anything incriminating. "I don't think Charles would keep anything related to the case right here in his desk. If it was me, I'd keep it in a bank deposit box, out of sight."

"Let's hope Charles doesn't think that way." Ynes let out a curse. "The safe won't open. I'll concentrate on the file cabinets."

Thirty minutes passed and Olivia had found nothing, when Ynes walked over to the desk with a photo album in her hands. "Look at this. It was at the bottom of one of the cabinets."

Olivia looked at the open album to see page after page of photographs of Ella Clinton Cohen. In some of them, Ynes was with her mother. In others, Ella and Charles were shown at home, at events, in the park, at the beach. "They looked happy together," Olivia said.

"Funny. I never realized how few photos Charles has on display in the house. I can only recall one of me and my mother in the music room."

"Maybe Charles really did love your mother. Maybe he had nothing to do with the heist." Olivia glanced at a small, pewter clock set on the desk. "And maybe we should get out of here before Charles gets back. It's getting late."

When Ynes lifted the album from the desk to return it to the file cabinet, three loose photographs slipped out from the back pages and fell to the floor. Ynes picked them up and as she was about to return them to the album, she glanced at the photographs and froze.

"Liv." With shaking fingers, Ynes put one of the pictures on the desk in front of her friend.

Olivia took a look and snatched up the photo to see it more closely. Making eye contact with Ynes, she handed it to her. "Put it back."

"Is it who I think it is?" Ynes sounded breathless.

"Yes." Olivia shoved the folders into the drawer and closed it. "It's Michael White, or whatever his name is."

The photo had shown a younger Michael White standing off to the side near a grove of trees. Ynes's stepfather was also in the photo. He wore a suit and stood with several other men, all of them holding drinks in their hands. It appeared to be a business event or function of some kind.

"There's a date on the back." Ynes did a quick calculation in her head. "It was taken when I was five. It was the month prior to the heist."

Olivia stood up, her heart pounding. "Put it back. Put the album back in the cabinet. We can't be caught looking at that picture." She adjusted the desk chair to the way it was when they came into the office. "We need to get out of here. Make sure everything is back the way we found it."

The young women listened at the door before opening it, heard nothing, and stepped out into the hall where they hurried away to the second floor.

Once in Ynes's room, Olivia spoke. "Charles knows Michael White. He's known him since before the heist."

Ynes sat on her bed, her hands on the sides of her face. "Charles must be involved. White must work for Charles. Oh, no," she moaned. "Oh, no."

"It might be a good idea for us to leave," Olivia said. "You can tell Charles we've had to change plans and have to return to Boston. Get your things ... or just leave them here for now. Take your laptop and your flash drives. Let's get out of here. Now."

Ynes slipped off the bed and knelt next to her suitcase to remove her laptop.

Footsteps could be heard in the hallway approaching Ynes's closed bedroom door.

A knock.

"Ynes?" It was Greta, the housekeeper. "Your father is home. He'd like you to meet him in the music room in fifteen minutes."

Ynes stared at the door, but didn't respond.

Olivia gestured at her friend to reply.

Ynes swallowed hard, her face beginning to pale. "Thank you, Greta. We'll be down shortly." Turning her eyes to Olivia, she whispered, "What are we going to do?"

32

"We're going down to the music room," Olivia said. "We're going to act normal, and then early tomorrow morning, we're going to leave."

"I feel ill." Ynes placed her hand on her stomach.

"Hide it." Before Olivia opened the door, she said, "We have no proof that Charles has done anything wrong. Just because he's in a photo with White standing nearby, it doesn't implicate him in the heist. Charles might not know White. It might be a coincidence that they were at the same event."

Ynes gave a shaky nod.

"Act normal," Olivia said and opened the door.

CHARLES TURNED AROUND and greeted the young

women when he heard them enter the room. He gave Ynes a hug. "I apologize for being so late. The meeting went on and on. Are you settled in?" he asked with a smile.

"We are," Olivia said. "Thank you for your hospitality."

"Are you feeling okay?" Charles looked at Ynes with concern.

"I might have a cold coming on. I'm fine." Ynes forced a smile.

"How about a little brandy then?" Charles poured some liquid into an elegant crystal glass for Ynes and after asking Olivia what she'd like, he handed her a wine glass of merlot. "I'm not sure Erik will join us. I haven't heard from him today."

After discussing his day at the office, Charles asked the young women about the research they were doing. "Have you made some headway?"

"Some." Ynes placed her glass on the coffee table.

"Are you able to share the information?"

Olivia looked over at Ynes who was staring at the floor with her hands clasped in her lap. "We've made some interesting connections," Olivia said to fill the silence.

"What sort of connections?" Charles swirled the dark liquid in his glass.

Before Olivia could respond, Ynes said, "Before we tell you what we've learned, can you tell us what you know about the heist?"

"I think I've told you all I know. There was some initial hope that the paintings would be found, but as time went on, it seemed more unlikely. I have heard that some serious negotiations are underway, but I've heard that before. We can be optimistic, I suppose."

Ynes asked, "What about the men involved in the heist? Is there any new information about them? Who they were? What their connections might be? Who masterminded the whole thing?"

"I haven't heard anything new."

"Do you know the name Pete Wall?" Ynes asked.

Olivia's heart sank as she looked quickly at Ynes before turning to catch Charles's reaction.

"I've heard that name, yes," Charles said softly.

"What did you hear about him?"

"He may have been one of the men who robbed the Cooper. I also read recently that the man is dead."

"Murdered," Ynes said. "How about Tobey Sewall? You've heard that name, too, haven't you?"

Charles spoke in a low tone. "I know the man gave the FBI some information. I know Sewall was distraught over Ella's murder and left the crime world behind. The FBI told me that."

"What about Ricky Spence?" Ynes asked. "Do you know that name?"

Charles sighed and took a sip of his drink. "A low-level mobster."

"Low-level mobsters seem to live pretty well."

Charles tilted his head. "What do you mean?"

"Did you know that Ricky Spence supposedly shot and killed my mother?"

Charles shook his head and adjusted in his seat. "I've heard many rumors from many different sources. I've never heard that one. I'd only heard he might have had something to do with the heist."

"Why didn't you tell me you'd heard his name?" Ynes bit her lip.

"There's no proof of anything," Charles said. "Why burden you with all of it? It's hard enough for me to listen to the possibilities and then have nothing come of them."

"Do you know a man named Michael White?" Ynes asked, her posture rigid.

Olivia pinned her gaze on Ynes's stepfather.

Charles considered the name. "I don't believe so. Who is he?"

Olivia flashed Ynes a look of warning. She did not want Ynes to accuse Charles. She did not want a confrontation with the man in his home, a confrontation she was afraid they might lose. "It's a name that came up in our research."

"I'm not familiar with it," Charles said.

Ynes leaned forward, her eyes wet. "Did you have anything to do with the heist? Did you have anything to do with my mother's death?"

Charles's eyes widened and he looked like he'd been struck. "No. No, Ynes. I loved your mother. Why on earth do you think such a terrible thing?"

Ynes closed her eyes. "Why did you fight with Erik that night? Why did you slap him?"

"Ynes." Just as Charles stood to go to her, Greta appeared at the entrance to the room.

"Excuse me. The call you've been waiting for came in." Greta glanced at Ynes. "Is there anything I can do before I leave for the night?"

Charles bent and gave Ynes a hug. "I have to take this call. I'll only be a short time. Then we need to have a long talk." He looked over at Olivia and nodded, and then he wished Greta good night before heading to his office to take the call.

The housekeeper left the room.

Olivia hurried to sit by her friend and she put her arm around her. "I'm not sure that was the right thing to do."

Ynes said, "I was about to burst. I couldn't take it any longer."

"I think Charles might be telling the truth," Olivia said.

Movement near the door to the living room made Olivia turn. Erik Cohen entered the music room.

"Sorry I'm late. Where's Dad?" Erik strode to the bar, poured himself a drink, and then leaned back against the glossy wood while he sipped. His expression looked agitated.

Ynes, surprised to see Erik, brushed at her cheeks, but didn't say anything.

"Your father went to take a call," Olivia said.

"How are things?" Erik asked as he went to the door leading to the hall and shut it.

Alarm bells went off inside Olivia's head and she stiffened. The blond hairs on her arms stood up.

"How's your research going?" Erik asked.

"Fine," Ynes said.

"Getting close to finding some answers?" Erik's manner was challenging.

"Possibly." Ynes eyed her stepbrother with suspicion.

"I heard you ask Dad about Michael White. I was in the living room listening to your conversation." An ugly smile formed over Erik's face.

Olivia stood up and glanced around for something to use as a weapon.

"Sit down," Erik growled.

Olivia didn't budge.

"What are you doing, Erik?" Ynes asked softly.

"What I should have done long before now. Getting rid of another loose end. You had to stick your nose into the past, didn't you? You had to try and figure it out." Erik's eyes were dark with hate. "You're not going to ruin my life."

The light dawned in Ynes's head. "Michael White works for *you*. What do you have to do with the heist? You had blood on your shirt that night when you came home." She narrowed her eyes. "What did you do?"

Erik smirked. "I was in on it. I drove the getaway car. At least, that was all I was supposed to do. The plans changed."

"What happened?" Ynes nearly hissed.

"Things got out of hand. You were right about Ricky Spence. He's the one who shot Ella. They called me on the walkie-talkie. I was out back waiting in the car for them to carry out the paintings. They told me to get inside. Both guards were on the floor when I got there."

"Spence killed her," Ynes muttered.

"Ella was still alive when I went in. She saw me."

"Did she speak?"

"She held her hand out to me."

"You went to her?"

Erik shook his head. "The guys told me to help cut the paintings out of the frames. We had to get the artwork and get out of there."

Ynes's face hardened and she jumped to her feet. She shrieked at Erik. "You let her die alone? You didn't try to help her? She was alive?"

Erik lunged at Olivia and wrapped his arm around her from the back. He pulled out a knife and held it to her throat. "Go to the carriage house, Ynes. Move or I'll kill your friend. Hurry up. Get going. Go out the living room way. I'm right behind you. Make one move and I'll slit her throat."

Olivia clutched at Erik's arm and made eye contact with Ynes, sending her a silent message.

"Move," Erik spit out the word.

Ynes started to walk, but swung around. Olivia

put her head forward to try to protect her throat and she used her heel to kick Erik in the knee.

Ynes crouched and moved her hands and feet so fast that they blurred as she pummeled her stepbrother.

Erik let Olivia go and as he whirled towards the door to the living room, a blast shook the room and the door from the hall flew open.

Charles rushed in, a gun in his hand. He had shot the lock out of the door.

Olivia and Ynes flinched thinking the man would turn the weapon on them, but Charles shouted at Erik to stop.

Erik bolted for the door to escape.

Another blast from Charles's gun and Erik fell to the floor screaming and grabbing at his leg. Blood seeped through the leg of Erik's trousers.

Charles stormed across the room. "I heard what you said, you bastard," he roared at Erik. "You let her bleed to death? You son of a bitch. You let Ella die? You let Ella die."

Charles pointed the gun at Erik's head, his hand shaking with rage.

"No!" Ynes dashed across the room. "No, Dad. Don't kill him." She grabbed Charles's arm. "Don't do it." Tears flowed down the young woman's cheeks. "He isn't worth it," she cried.

Staring at Erik writhing on the floor, Charles dropped his arm.

Olivia took the gun away from him and walked to the landline phone behind the bar to make the emergency call.

Charles Cohen wrapped Ynes in his arms, and the two wept.

33

E rik Cohen was hauled away from the mansion in an ambulance. Olivia and Charles had tended to the bullet wound in Erik's leg by wrapping a towel around it and pressing lightly to stay the bleeding. Charles had moved like a zombie, with an expression as hard as stone.

Ynes had stood off to the side, shaking, her arms crossed over her chest, watching the proceedings. When the police arrived, each person was questioned, the knife and Charles's gun were taken, and photographs of the scene were snapped.

Olivia, Ynes, and Charles sat in the living room together while the crime scene investigators continued their work.

"I didn't know," Charles shook his head. "I

should have. Erik came home late that night. He had blood on his shirt. He told me he had been in a fight. He smelled of weed, his breath reeked of alcohol." Charles let out a breath. "I'd just received the call about Ella ... and that young fool waltzed around the house like an idiot. When I told him about the call from the police, he made some flip remark. I slapped him across the face."

"I saw the slap. I heard something about my mother. I'd seen Erik come in when he walked past my room. I saw the blood on his shirt. It scared me. He made some rude remarks to me as he walked by," Ynes said.

"I'll never forget the horror of that night," Charles said. His bloodshot eyes stared across the room at nothing. "My Ella ... gone." After a few moments, Charles said, "Erik had always been difficult, got into trouble, was disagreeable, aggressive. He rarely showed empathy for anyone or anything. I didn't know how to handle him. I was distraught over Ella. I was numb for months and months and retreated into my work, the one thing I knew how to handle, the one thing I could control."

Ynes reached over and took her stepfather's hand.

"Erik was involved in the heist?" A few tears

tumbled down the man's cheeks. "I knew he was in with a bad crowd, but hardened criminals, the mob? I can't comprehend it." Charles held tight to Ynes's hand. "He let Ella die. He didn't try to help her. I don't know how to ever forgive him."

Later that night, Olivia dragged herself up to the guest room and made a call to Brad to tell him what had happened. He asked a million questions, and despite her exhaustion, she answered every one. Just hearing Brad's voice was a comfort.

"I'll come down early tomorrow to meet you," he told you.

Olivia protested saying he didn't need to come all that way and she would take the train back, but Brad insisted. "Of course, I'm going to come. I should be there right now with you."

"I wish you were here." Olivia slurred her words from fatigue. "I want to be home."

Ricky Spence and Pete Wall worked in Jimmy Faber's gang and had been the two men who robbed the Cooper Museum of the artwork. Erik Cohen was to be the driver of the getaway car along with Adam Mack. Tim Mack, the Cooper guard, refused to allow his brother to be involved in the heist so Erik handled the task himself. Erik was called into the museum to assist with removing the paintings from their frames and transporting them to the car.

When Erik arrived in the museum, he saw the two guards on the floor, bleeding from gunshot wounds. Tim Mack was unconscious, but Ella was still alive and reached out to Erik when she saw him enter the room.

Erik ignored her and let her bleed to death. He was afraid if she lived, she would report his part in the heist to the police. Ricky Spence told Erik he knew Ella was his stepmother. He couldn't allow her to live to speak to the police. She would have told them Erik was involved in the robbery and then Erik would rat them out.

Michael White's real name was David Lincoln. He'd worked in security and came highly recommended so Charles Cohen hired the man to accompany Erik to the outdoor adventure program in order to keep his son in line and to make sure he completed the ten-month course. David Lincoln also remained on Charles's payroll for the four years of Erik's undergraduate degree. Lincoln was hired to keep Erik out of trouble and to make sure he finished the degree program and graduated from college.

Charles had not counted on the two men becoming friends. Neither did he expect Erik to hire David Lincoln as his own thug who would do anything Erik asked him to do, including attacking Tilly, planning to kill Abigail Millett on the very day Ricky Spence got to her, and murdering Ricky Spence.

Erik's plans to run for public office would not be ruined by the past events of his life ... and he would do anything necessary to keep it that way.

The recent negotiations for the safe return of the paintings to the Cooper had caused concern in the criminal underworld. The police wanted the name of the person who had killed Ella Cohen, but the crime bosses had no intention of giving up the name of the killer.

When Pete Wall went to talk with Abigail Millett, ripples of concern wound its way through the network of mobsters. He had to be taken out. When Ricky Spence took it upon himself to murder Wall and Abigail Millett, he overstepped into territory he had no business in. He paid with his life.

Michael White was not part of the gangs whose job it was to mete out punishment, and so for killing Spence under Erik's orders, White met his unnatural fate one week after Erik Cohen took the ambulance ride from his father's mansion to the hospital.

Turf wars had broken out in the city as the mobsters jockeyed for position within the crime circles, but things would be settled and quiet within a month. Unfortunately, the negotiations for the artwork were impacted and once again, no deal was made and the paintings were not returned to the Cooper.

The exact charges the district attorney's office would level against Erik Cohen were unclear, but Charles and Ynes believed the man would be put away for many, many years.

Ynes thanked the fates every day that she and Olivia had escaped her stepbrother's plans to kill them. Erik had worried that Ynes's research would point to him and she would eventually recall what he'd said to her when he came home the night Ella was murdered, and that she would link him to the heist.

Ynes stayed in Boston for another week and then returned to England to work on the final year of her graduate degree.

Before Ynes went through airport security on the way back to London, she embraced Olivia for several long minutes. "You're the most loyal and amazing friend anyone could ask for."

"If you need me, I'm there," Olivia smiled. "I know you'd do the same for me. Just stay out of trouble for a while, will you? I don't need any more excitement for a long time."

"How about I stay out of trouble for the rest of my life?" Ynes asked.

"That works for me." Olivia looked her friend in the eye. "You and Charles are making progress on repairing your relationship?"

"I think I'd call it, *forging* a relationship."

"You called him "dad" the night Erik attacked us," Olivia pointed out.

"I know." Ynes nodded. "In fact, I've called him that several more times since that night."

"I bet he's happy about that." Olivia touched her friend's arm.

"I'm happy about it, too. He's coming to visit me in Oxford next week."

Olivia smiled to hear that news, but then her expression turned serious. "Your mother's killer will never serve prison time. I'm sorry you didn't get the justice you hoped for."

"I think I got something more important out of all this ... and I think it would make my mother very happy," Ynes said. "It seems that now, I have a father." She hugged her friend tight and hurried to get through the security line in time to make her flight.

Olivia watched her go and then headed away to leave the terminal to call for a car to take her back to the Boston hotel she and Brad were staying in for two nights. Reaching into her bag for her phone, she saw a white envelope in the side pocket.

When she removed it and found the note inside, she recognized her friend's handwriting.

I promised you a tropical vacation after all of this was over. You thought I'd forget, didn't you? Since I have to be at Oxford for the term, I don't think Brad would mind taking my place as your travel companion. Enjoy. Love you.

Attached to the letter was a voucher from a travel agency for a one-week all-expenses paid trip to Hawaii for two people.

Olivia held the letter to her chest and as her eyes misted over, she let out a happy whoop of gratitude ... and then she slunk away out of the terminal when people turned and scowled at her for her outburst.

~

Olivia and Brad stood inside the store together.

"Ready?" Olivia asked. "It's your first game."

"Here you go." Brad handed the man the noise-cancelling headphones.

Randy, wearing a Red Sox t-shirt, looked tentatively at the headphones. He didn't like a lot of noise so Olivia suggested he wear his earbuds attached to his phone so he could listen to his favorite radio announcer during the game, but could be in the stands for the first time to watch.

"Did you put in your earbuds?" Olivia stepped forward. "Okay, now let's put the headphones over your head. There. Now you can listen to the game, block out all the extra noise, and see the field and the players in person. Are you ready to do it?"

Randy beamed at Olivia and gave her a thumbs-up sign.

"This is a big playoff game," Olivia told the man. "The team needs their number one fan in the stands to cheer them."

With a wide smile, Paulina walked beside them as they left the leather store with Randy in between Olivia and Brad, holding tightly to their hands.

Throngs of people moved over the sidewalks, a band played on the outside patio of a restaurant, and the four of them walked through the turnstiles and entered the ball park. With the sun low in the sky, they made their way up the ramp and came out by the infield grandstands, the emerald green field stretching out before them under the brightest of lights.

Randy gasped and stood as still as a statue taking in the dazzling sight of the field, the players, and the stands filled with people.

Suddenly, he turned to Olivia with a mile-wide grin and wrapped her in a bear hug, almost lifting her off her feet.

Brad put his hand gently on Randy's shoulder. "It's only the beginning of a great night, big guy. Let's go take our seats."

Olivia smiled at Brad's kind manner and she reached her hand out for his, so grateful and happy they were together. "I really missed you those two weeks," she whispered. "I'm glad you're with me again."

"With you is the only place I ever want to be." Brad leaned down and kissed her, and his lips touching hers sent little sparks of heat jumping around in Olivia's heart.

THANK YOU FOR READING!

To hear about new books and book sales, please sign
up for my mailing list at:
www.jawhitingbooks.com

Your email will never be sold, shared, or spammed.

If you enjoyed the book, please consider leaving a
review. A few lines are all that's needed. It would be
very much appreciated.

ALSO BY J.A. WHITING

OLIVIA MILLER MYSTERIES

SWEET COVE COZY MYSTERIES

LIN COFFIN COZY MYSTERIES

CLAIRE ROLLINS COZY MYSTERIES

PAXTON PARK COZY MYSTERIES

ABOUT THE AUTHOR

J.A. Whiting lives with her family in Massachusetts. Whiting loves reading and writing mystery and suspense stories.

Visit / follow me at:
www.jawhitingbooks.com
www.bookbub.com/authors/j-a-whiting
www.amazon.com/author/jawhiting
www.facebook.com/jawhitingauthor